'How can I bel[ieve you] planned to come [back] years ago and me[et as] arranged?

'Especially if you married someone else a month later?' Luke's grip on Ellie's shoulders tightened.

Ellie's teeth were gritted. 'Your mother told me you were married. You can believe me, or her. That's your choice. I'm sorry, but maybe it's all for the best anyway. Who knows? It's in the past.'

She wriggled out of his grasp and faced him. 'If I'd come back here I wouldn't have had Josh, and I could never regret my son in my life.' She stepped back a pace. 'But at this moment I regret you in my life.'

Luke flinched, and then his arms shot out again as he pulled Ellie towards him. 'Then regret this, too!'

And his lips came down and captured hers...

Fiona McArthur is Australian and lives with her husband and five sons on the Mid-North coast of New South Wales. Her interests are writing, reading, playing tennis, e-mail and discovering the fun of computers—of course that's when she's not watching the boys play competition cricket, football or tennis. She loves her work as part-time midwife in a country hospital, facilitates antenatal classes and enjoys the company of young mothers in a teenage pregnancy group.

Fiona McArthur's website can be viewed at: fionamcarthur.com

Recent titles by the same author:

EMERGENCY IN MATERNITY
THE MIDWIFE'S SECRET
FATHER IN SECRET
MIDWIFE UNDER FIRE
DELIVERING LOVE

DELIVERING SECRETS

BY
FIONA McARTHUR

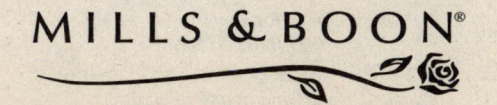

MILLS & BOON

To my wonderful sons:
Stewart, Rohan, Andrew, Scott and Rory.

DID YOU PURCHASE THIS BOOK WITHOUT A COVER?

If you did, you should be aware it is **stolen property** as it was reported
unsold and destroyed by a retailer. Neither the author nor the publisher
has received any payment for this book.

All the characters in this book have no existence outside the imagination of the author, and have no relation whatsoever to anyone bearing the same name or names. They are not even distantly inspired by any individual known or unknown to the author, and all the incidents are pure invention.

All Rights Reserved including the right of reproduction in whole or in part in any form. This edition is published by arrangement with Harlequin Enterprises II B.V. The text of this publication or any part thereof may not be reproduced or transmitted in any form or by any means, electronic or mechanical, including photocopying, recording, storage in an information retrieval system, or otherwise, without the written permission of the publisher.

This book is sold subject to the condition that it shall not, by way of trade or otherwise, be lent, resold, hired out or otherwise circulated without the prior consent of the publisher in any form of binding or cover other than that in which it is published and without a similar condition including this condition being imposed on the subsequent purchaser.

*MILLS & BOON and MILLS & BOON with the Rose Device
are registered trademarks of the publisher.*

*First published in Great Britain 2003
Harlequin Mills & Boon Limited,
Eton House, 18-24 Paradise Road, Richmond, Surrey TW9 1SR*

© Fiona McArthur 2003

ISBN 0 263 83440 9

*Set in Times Roman 10½ on 12 pt.
03-0403-51168*

*Printed and bound in Spain
by Litografia Rosés, S.A., Barcelona*

CHAPTER ONE

ELLIE glared at herself in the rear-view mirror. She'd never fit in as a clinic nurse, and what made her think Luke Farrell would talk to her—let alone give her a job? Until she'd moved back here last week, she'd thought he was married so she hadn't come back to the small seaside town, once she'd qualified as a midwife, as she'd promised Luke she would all those years ago!

She'd only lived in Bell's Creek for a summer when she was seventeen. And that pact they'd made had been a romantic teenage whim.

For most of Ellie's childhood, her mother had breezed into a town, stayed a short while and breezed out. Ellie had learned not to pine over lost friends but she'd never been able to forget Luke Farrell.

Ellie clutched her handbag as if it were her talisman and climbed out of the old Volvo. If she was going to make a go of this fresh start then a new job was a necessity. She had to pay the bills.

Her skills and qualifications weren't a problem. It was just desperation that made her panic so much about getting this job with Luke—nothing to do with the past. Shoulders straight, she pushed open the door and superglued a smile on to her face. Be confident!

The prune-faced receptionist glanced up and her eyes widened under black-rimmed glasses. Ellie decided it was either her very short hair—she'd shaved her head for Leukaemia Week a few months before—or because her belly was flat. Maybe you needed a pregnancy to qualify to come in here?

The receptionist's cold glance travelled down to the brown skin between Ellie's low-slung trousers and the beaded hem of her midriff top. She sniffed. Ellie mentally shrugged, immune to sniffers.

'Hi. I'm Ellie Diamond. I've an interview with Dr Farrell at one o'clock.'

The receptionist shifted her gaze to a point over Ellie's left shoulder. 'Please, take a seat, Ms Diamond. I'll let Doctor know you're here. He will be with you as soon as he can.'

Ellie smiled politely back. 'It's Mrs Diamond, and thank you.' And that tells me nothing about how long. Ellie resigned herself to a wait as she sank into one of the comfortably padded chairs between two young pregnant women. A painting glared at her from the wall. She forced her fingers to relax on her handbag as she considered Luke Farrell's choice in art.

The painting was quite the ugliest wall adornment she'd ever seen. All reds and greens and white, slashed to form a portrait of a woman—at least, Ellie thought it was a woman, but it was hard to tell. It was an original and probably very expensive. She sighed. Her late husband, Steve, had said she had no appreciation for abstract art. But, then, she liked things to be vibrant and warm, not just a good investment.

The heavy wooden door to the consulting room opened silently to allow a tiny Asian woman into the waiting room. Her belly poked imperiously forward through the silk of her dress. Then Luke walked out and Ellie felt seventeen again.

The years had taken any softness from around Luke's jaw and cheekbones, and had radiated fine lines from the corners of his beautiful eyes, but he was still well muscled and dark-haired. He said goodbye to the pregnant woman and his smile was the same—warm and genuine. It bounced off the walls of the room and even the painting looked better.

Luke would always be able to sell toothpaste—or bed linen!

Ellie's hand surreptitiously felt for the pulse-volume increase in her wrist. Yep. She was having palpitations from a man she hadn't seen for more than ten years. So much for maturity.

Dr Farrell glanced around the room until he found the girl next to Ellie. 'Ms Keys, please, come through.' His voice was slow and deep and the young lady blushed and hastened to her feet.

His glance passed over Ellie and then froze briefly as his slashing black brows furrowed for a moment and his eyes burned into hers. He looked away and Ellie felt as if she'd been pigeonholed for later. The door shut behind them and it was as if the room became ordinary again.

Ellie frowned. She'd forgotten the effect Luke had had on her. From the distance of Sydney she'd gradually decided her attraction to him had been overrated, a teenage infatuation. From that one glance she could remember the colour of his eyes, the curve of his nose and the strength of his chin, and a hell of a lot of other things!

She forced herself to shrug. To look cost nothing, but she'd never been in the same league as Luke Farrell. Laid-back Steve had been more her style and his death had scared her more than she'd thought possible. To get involved with a man could ruin your life. And she wasn't putting herself or Josh through that heartbreak again.

It took another twenty minutes before the waiting room

was empty except for Ellie. When the outside door shut on the final client Luke gestured her in.

Ellie slipped in front of him and she couldn't help but appreciate that he was a good head taller than her own five feet six. It was kind of nice in a you-make-me-feel-feminine way.

When Luke had shut the door, he held out his hand. 'Thank you for coming, Ms Diamond,' he said formally.

Ellie met his eyes. 'It's *Mrs* Diamond. I'm a widow.'

He broke eye contact and all he said was, 'My condolences.' Ellie looked down at his hand and warily put her fingers in his. Bad mistake. His grip was like a homecoming, safe and warm and caring, and she didn't want to let go. She forced her fingers to drop his hand and almost fell into the chair he indicated. Her knuckles were white again on the handle of her handbag.

Luckily, he didn't seem to notice anything strange in her behaviour. His expression was polite and interested. Ellie could see he'd perfected the art of listening.

He'd always been one of those people who made you feel a ridiculous urge to confess all sins and bemoan what a cruel world it was. Ellie suppressed the impulse. She needed some direction here. It must be time to pull the résumé from her hand bag.

Her credentials were crumpled at the edges, and she smoothed the papers a little before she placed then on the desk. She recited her latest confidence mantra under her breath. You are a great midwife. He would be lucky to have you. The silence stretched on and Ellie had to break it. She drew a deep breath and smiled shakily.

'Thank you for seeing me, Dr Farrell. Luke. You have a lovely surgery here.' She felt inane but at least she was trying.

Luke almost sighed with regret. Lord, how he'd loved

her all those years ago. Her voice still sounded the same as it always had—beautifully melodic, like the rhythmic beat of the waves he could hear at night in his bed. He frowned at the fanciful thought. He didn't have fanciful thoughts about women in this office, and he'd stopped fantasising about Ellie McGuire ten years ago.

Or at least in the five since she'd failed to make good on their pact to return to Bell's River. To make matters worse, Ellie hadn't even had the decency to tell him herself that she wouldn't be coming back. She'd left a message with his mother instead. Since then, Luke had decided that was all for the best. But why did she have to come back now?

He stared down at the papers but didn't pick them up. He was at a loss to know how to interview her. Apart from the fact that he wasn't masochistic enough to want to work with the only woman he'd offered his heart to, she was the direct opposite to what he'd had in mind for his obstetric practice.

He'd envisaged a middle aged, soft-spoken, motherly woman available to take the blood-pressure checks and urine testing off his hands. And hopefully provide a sympathetic ear to problems that his clients were often reluctant to discuss with a male doctor.

What he had in front of him was a woman from his past, whom he'd finally not thought of for a reasonable length of time.

Admittedly she looked different to the seventeen-year-old he remembered. Apart from the fact that she now wore her stunning fiery red hair in a short crop, the years had only fulfilled the promise of her youth.

Ellie's skin was still that pale peach that should have burned in the sun but didn't seem to, and if she had lines on her face, they were too fine for him to see. With her pert breasts and those long legs, she was even more gut-wrenchingly beautiful.

He wasn't into gorgeous radicals with cutely cropped hair and lots of jewellery—so why did he feel like he was suffering from a sudden attack of asthma?

A sardonic voice inside his head whispered that there was no breathlessness when his fiancée, Anthea, walked into the room.

Luke leaned across the desk and picked up Ellie's résumé to distract his disloyal thoughts. Midwifery, Advanced Life Support Obstetrics, Neonatal Intensive Care, two years each at three different hospitals—so she still moved around a lot.

Little Ellie had done well with her midwifery, he mused. Her credentials were impressive. Emotionally he could never judge this woman fairly, but morally he should consider her. 'So what brings you back to Bell's River, Ellie McGuire?' He didn't add 'five years too late', but he felt like it and the bitterness tasted like flat beer on his tongue.

With Luke's use of her maiden name Ellie sighed. 'I moved here a week ago.' She shrugged. 'I have some great memories from here.'

Uncharacteristically, she avoided his eyes and he would have loved to have known what she was thinking.

'My husband died four years ago from leukaemia and I want to settle somewhere near the sea.' She'd always loved the sea, and he'd always fantasised about making love with Ellie behind one of the dunes out past the cove. Bare skin and sea breeze...

Then she added, 'I have a four-year-old son.'

She'd married someone else rather than fulfil her promise to him, and had borne that man a son. Both facts twisted the knife in a wound he'd thought healed. His attention slid between her top and her low-slung trousers. Her belly was brown and flat, unmarred by any sign of the past pregnancy.

Luke fought the images that formed when he looked at her. Once he'd dreamed of Ellie and their children, but that's what he'd been doing—dreaming.

He gritted his teeth. She'd always confused the hell out of him, but he felt a little better when he realised she was nervous, too. She absent-mindedly twisted the silver ring that adorned her left hand. So Ellie was uncomfortable. Good.

'But why this position, Ellie?' He couldn't bring himself to call her Mrs Diamond. 'You always wanted to be a hands-on midwife. Surely a hospital setting would suit your experience better.' Then he cursed himself for admitting to remembering things about her.

Haunting, almond-shaped eyes met his gaze. She made him think of their special cove—and the pact—and tanned skin on tanned skin. And especially the time she'd offered herself to him there and he'd stopped at the last moment with some notion of her being too young and his fear of consequences.

'The hospital can only offer me casual work. I'm a good midwife,' she said, and her voice flowed across the desk and wrapped around his shoulders like a ghost from his past. 'I care about women. I'm interested in antenatal care and that a woman should have the best birth experience that she can possibly have. I want to do what I can to help that happen.'

Her voice ebbed and rolled and he could have listened to her all day if he could just leave his eyes shut and remember what she used to look like with her long wavy red hair and bare feet.

Then she brought him back to the present with a thud when she added, 'And I need a job.'

There was no doubting the tinge of desperation in her voice or in her words. Especially the last sentence. He stifled the urge to help her. 'I'm sorry, Ellie. I can see from your experience and references that you do care for women, and I'm sure whoever employs you next will be very fortunate to have you, but I was looking for someone more motherly.'

Her green eyes looked defeated for a moment and then they darkened to the purple-green of threatening hail clouds. He could almost sniff the brine of an impending storm and it was something he'd forgotten she was capable of. She didn't often fire up but when she did there was hell to pay. Even her voice was more substantial. 'I am a mother, Luke Farrell. My son is four years old. You can't get more motherly than that. It's my appearance, isn't it?'

He winced at her directness but she was partly right. 'It's the whole package, Ellie. But the hairstyle, certainly jumps out at one.' He admitted to a curious fascination and the interview was a shambles anyway. 'What on earth made you cut your hair so short?'

'I was sponsored to shave it a while ago.' She shrugged and ran her hand through her close-cropped hair. 'To raise money for leukaemia research. I don't regret it, just wish it would grow faster perhaps.' She gathered up her papers.

When she stood up, her bare stomach was at Luke's eye level and he felt his lips twitch. Ellie had always enjoyed wearing unconventional clothes but he couldn't really think of a less suitable outfit for a job interview. It was so typical of her.

Ellie lifted her hand in a tiny salute, a gesture he remembered from the old days, and his heart squeezed. Now he felt that he'd been dismissed instead of the other way around. She didn't offer her hand and he missed the contact. And he didn't like the way he'd prejudged her application. Luke tried to envisage her in some sort of corporate uniform with maybe smaller earrings and no necklaces. It was hard.

He found himself standing, too—irresistibly drawn to the cliff-edge of spending more time with her. 'Look, Ellie...' He glanced at his watch. He had an hour before the next patient was due. 'Maybe I haven't given you a fair go. I have a standing reservation for lunch at a restaurant in town—would you like to join me? You're welcome to come and try and convince me that you would be an asset in this practice.'

Ellie's first impulse was to give him a crisp 'no, thank you', but the unpaid bills would still be on the kitchen table when she went home. She had that vague promise of casual shifts at the local maternity unit but that was only if someone was off sick or left. Her mother had taught her it wasn't nice to pray for the plague—or stay around to catch it.

And maybe she did look a bit scary, to someone as strait-laced as Luke Farrell had always been. She had the feeling that this was a bad idea anyway. She sighed and nodded. 'OK. But no restaurant—you can buy me a hamburger next door.'

He blinked and then smiled, and in Ellie's mind the room faded under the direct wattage. 'You're on.'

Luke watched her wrestle with the huge hamburger. Ellie's long fingers were splayed as she tried to hold the rapidly disintegrating bread roll together in a losing battle. A browned pineapple ring threatened to slide sideways into her lap and the beetroot darkened the pink of her lips as she caught it just before it skidded out between the shredded lettuce and the egg.

He suppressed a smile. He rarely ate here because they didn't give you a knife and fork and you needed a bath after eating the big hamburgers. But Ellie had always preferred take-aways to dining in. Ten years ago she'd rather have had the cove and hot chips to a night out at the local restaurant.

She had her elbows on the table as she tried to narrow the field of the mess. 'Why didn't you warn me about this burger?' She glared at him and this time he did smile.

'And miss the show?' He shook his head and she smiled wryly back at him.

'So, is this convincing you to give me the job?' She took another bite and concentrated on finishing her lunch.

Luke sat back in his chair and looked at her, not at the woman-package of her because that was too distracting, but the half-hidden laughter in her eyes and the warmth and zest for life that she'd always shown. 'How reliable are you?' The words came out more harshly than he'd intended. He didn't say, You didn't come back when you were supposed to, last time, but it was there in the air between them.

He watched her attention flick back to him and, because she didn't have a hand to save it with, a piece of tomato slid from the side of the roll and fell onto her bare stomach. Without thought he pulled a serviette from the dispenser and scooped it gently off her stomach. She shivered beneath his fingers and he winced. He didn't have the right to do that.

Ellie put down the remains of the hamburger and pushed the plate away, as if her appetite had deserted her. She snagged her own serviette and patted her mouth and fingers. There was a tiny tremor in her voice but he couldn't tell if it was due to distress or anger. 'What makes you think *I'm* unreliable?'

'Let's just say past experience.' She frowned and before she could answer he brushed his comment aside. 'But you seem to have good references, which don't indicate a problem with your working life.'

'Gee, thanks.' Ellie scowled at him. 'So how about you tell me what else you want from your practice nurse if she can guarantee reliability?'

He ticked them off his fingers. 'Respectability or at least some degree of conventionality.' He raised his eyebrows once before going on as if to say, You may have a problem there. 'Empathy with my clients, experience in midwifery, including antenatal and postnatal care of women and their babies, computer skills and the ability to liaise with the hospital and other medical professionals.'

'So the job's right up my alley.' Ellie pinned him with a direct look. 'What's your major problem, Luke? What I look like or the fact it's me?'

He didn't answer but he knew that, except for the first point, he'd just described her. She would do the job well.

She shook her head. 'I guess that answers it. I'm the problem.' She stood up. 'Thanks for the burger.'

'Ellie, wait.' Luke stood up as well. He sighed. 'I'll give you a three-month trial period—but we're talking corporate dress code here. Monday, Tuesday, Wednesday eight-thirty to five-thirty. I don't need you on the other two days as Thursdays I'm operating all day and Friday is my gynaecological clinic at the hospital. Will the long days be all right for your son?'

Ellie smiled up at him. 'No worries. Three long days are better than five shorter days away from him.'

She stepped closer and took his hand to shake it. 'Thanks, Luke. You won't regret giving me a chance.'

She felt fragile beneath his fingers and he wanted to do more than shake hands with her. He disentangled himself before he acted on that impulse, then stepped back and glanced around the empty café. Only the proprietor was watching.

'I'll see you Monday, then,' he said, and walked quickly away.

CHAPTER TWO

ELLIE sat in her car and rested her head on the steering-wheel. She had a job. And the name of a place to buy a work outfit that covered her stomach.

She was exhausted and couldn't believe how much it had affected her, just seeing Luke. Age and experience had hardened the angles of his face but his innate kindness still shone through. But she hated the way that seeing Luke had brought back the memories of the past.

Ellie's mother had told her on her seventeenth birthday that she'd be completing her last year of high school in another town. She'd rushed off to Luke's house but he hadn't been there, only his mother. And the old witch had practically danced on the roof to hear that Ellie was leaving. Ellie shrugged off the pinprick of hurt from so long ago and concentrated on the present.

Well, at least for the three-month trial, she and Josh wouldn't go hungry. Not that Josh ate much. She frowned. And even less lately. She herself could live on a lettuce leaf. Ellie started the car and pulled out behind the only other car on the road—not exactly a stream of traffic.

She'd forgotten how quiet this small seaside town had been. And it hadn't changed much. She'd never really spent much time in the real inner Sydney, but the outer suburb where she'd spent the last year was an excited ants' nest compared to sleepy Bell's River.

The name Bell's River was music to Ellie's ears and she'd always envisaged it was because the mouth of the river was shaped like a bell as it merged with the sea. Then there was the cove. She'd loved the cove.

A few minutes later she pulled up at her rented house. It was small and quaint and in need of a birthday, but Ellie adored the disarray of it. The yard out back, with its big mulberry tree and run-down vegetable patch from previous tenants, was a wonderland for the garden enthusiast in Ellie.

But best of all was the delightful elderly couple next door who had offered to watch Josh for her any time, because they missed their own grandchildren.

When she knocked on the neighbour's door she could hear Josh gurgling with laughter from inside. It made all the struggles and the pain worthwhile to hear that sound, and she was still smiling when Lil Judd opened the door.

'Come in, Ellie. That boy of yours has had us in fits for the last hour.' Her friendly face peered up at Ellie. 'Did you get the job?'

Ellie grinned. 'Yep. Three days a week. I start on Monday, so I've a few days to get myself organised and Josh into preschool. Thanks for having him.'

'He's a pleasure, my dear. Josh's manners are beautiful and my man is here to help me. They're already great mates.'

Clem Judd looked up from the game of snakes and ladders and groaned at his miniature opponent's luck.

'Mum.' Josh caught sight of his favourite person and jumped up to wrap himself around his mother's legs. She stroked his head and then bent down to drop a kiss on his thatch of thick red hair because she couldn't help herself.

'Hello, my love. We have to go shopping. Have you had a good time?'

He nodded enthusiastically, grabbed his mother's hand and waved a cheery goodbye to the older couple.

Ellie managed to enrol Josh into a progressive pre-school with long day care to cover her work hours. She left Josh there for an hour to see if he liked it while she went uniform hunting.

Deciding on uniforms was a little harder. Luke Farrell must have forewarned the shop owner because there was a collection of skirts and tops waiting in the cubicle when she said who she was.

She hated all of them. Beige shirts, bottle green, fawn, pastel green, pastel yellow and pink. They were not Ellie's colours!

Ellie glanced at the woman's name badge. 'Susan, I can handle the bottle-green skirt but the beige shirt sucks. What else can we do?' She grinned down at the tiny saleswoman and the serious expression on the woman's face melted into a smile.

'I've a bright button-through top that would look lovely, and even a floral bottle green that would just stretch to sit over the waist of the skirt—but it's a bit see-through and you'd have to wear a flesh-coloured bra underneath. They're different but you'd still get away with looking corporate. They're only a little dearer but I'm sure Luke won't mind.'

The smile on Ellie's face faltered. 'Aren't I paying for these?'

Susan's eyes widened. 'Luke said to bill the surgery. I thought they were uniforms and I know the hospital supplies the uniforms there.'

Ellie wasn't sure what it was that made her uneasy but figuring out how to pay this off her credit card now wasn't a problem. She shrugged. 'You're a lifesaver,

Susan. In that case, I'll take them both and go look for some "corporate" shoes.'

'And stockings?' Susan was looking at her under her brows as if she were a recalcitrant child. Ellie burst out laughing and when she had herself back under control she murmured, 'In this heat? I don't think so.' She grinned again. 'Maybe those little sock things that sit inside your shoes.'

Susan shook her head and suggested the shoe store two doors down.

Back at the preschool to pick up Josh, Ellie smiled. 'You are amazing, Mr Diamond.' The stiffness in her neck eased when she saw how settled Josh was. The school was close to her work, which meant she could even walk to visit him in her lunch-hour. She hugged him and silently hoped that she would fit as well into her new job.

By the time Ellie had finished all her errands, Josh was wilting. 'Hungry, honey?' Josh shook his head. 'You've been such a good boy. Let's grab some take-aways to celebrate Mummy's new job.' She'd budget tomorrow. Monday would come around soon enough.

When Ellie walked into the surgery on Monday morning, recognition slid like a stiletto under Luke's ribs and made him wish he'd never hired her.

She looked fabulous. Different to the Ellie he remembered—but fabulous. The calf-length skirt showed her trim ankles to perfection and her stockings seemed the same colour as her skin. His eyes widened at the soft material of her bright orange shirt because it outlined her pert breasts in startling detail. She was corporate but with a wolf-whistle attached.

She'd thinned the silverware around her neck down to

one big crucifix, and the large hoops in her ears had been replaced by tiny studs. Luke sighed with relief. 'Good morning, Ellen.'

'Good morning, Luke. And it's still Ellie.' He couldn't help smiling back at her when she grinned, and suddenly his choice didn't seem so bad.

In the fifteen minutes before the first patient was due, Luke showed her how to open client files on the computer and record information in the database. The nurse's room, which would be hers to do her observations like blood pressures and weights, was small but workable. Then he formally introduced her to the unflappable June at the front desk explaining that June had been the practice receptionist in his father's day, too. The two women bared teeth at each other and Luke tried not to notice.

Ellie turned back to face him. 'I've typed out an introduction to give to your clients. Is that OK?'

She handed him an A4 sheet folded in two and his eyes were drawn to her beautiful hands. She had long, slender fingers and he could imagine how healing they would feel against a patient's skin—anyone's skin, in fact. He slid his finger under his collar and suddenly wondered if the air-conditioner was working. He reached across to dial the temperature down another degree.

Ellie rolled her eyes and he wrenched his mind back to the job on hand. 'I'd like you to read it,' she said. She didn't quite put her hands on her hips and Luke's lips twitched at her impatience.

She went on. 'If you're happy with it, perhaps June could photocopy some and give them out to the ladies as they come in.' He nodded and glanced down at the sheet, but she was still speaking.

'Otherwise your clients won't understand why they

don't see you first. I'd hate to be thought of as a necessary evil they had to pass to get to you.'

'Call them patients—I hate the word client,' Luke said absently. He didn't see her grimace as he took the paper and scanned the friendly message she'd prepared. It was good, concise yet informative, and she had a few things on there that he hadn't thought of as part of her role.

Her interests were listed: Birth plan discussion; questions from previous labours; natural remedies, and options in natural pain relief. He couldn't find fault with the paper even though it made him a little uneasy. He'd have to keep an eye on her but he had a suspicion the women would love it. It was a shame he had this crawling feeling of impending doom.

'I'd like to discuss some of these ideas as we get time through the day.' He looked at her from under his brows. 'You will remember this is my practice, won't you? Most of this seems fine. We'll see how it goes.' He smiled his killer smile as his first patient came through the front door.

'Good morning, Mrs Reece. I'll be with you in a couple of minutes.' He turned to introduce Ellie. 'This is Ellie. She's a midwife and is going to be adding a midwife's perspective along with mine for your antenatal care. Ellie's available for any questions and you'll see her first then I'll call you through for your usual visit.'

Ellie and Mrs Reece found themselves ushered towards the two chairs in the nurse's consulting room, and then Luke was gone. The two women looked at each other and Ellie grinned. 'Hi.' Mrs Reece smiled shyly back and Ellie knew it was going to OK.

By lunchtime, Ellie was exhausted, mostly from promoting herself and the benefits the women should expect by spending some time antenatally with a midwife. The actual work Luke wanted her to do while she was there was constant but easy. But the most draining part was an awareness of her ridiculous attraction to Luke Farrell which kept her on edge. The morning passed quickly and they never did get time to talk about her ideas.

Luckily, by the time she'd shared her lunch with Josh at his preschool, she was ready to face the afternoon appointments again. She clicked opened the appointment list on the screen and the next name jumped out at her. Belinda Farrell.

Maybe it was a coincidence but Farrell wasn't a common name. Ellie called up the pregnancy list and checked the due date, patient's age and present gestation of pregnancy.

From something her neighbour Lil Judd had said, Ellie now knew that while Luke had never been married, he was engaged to a midwife from the hospital. That was a different story to the one Luke's mother had told Ellie in that shattering phone call five years ago. Ellie shook off the disturbing memories and subsequent turn her life had taken, and tried to concentrate.

So Belinda Farrell would most likely be a relative of Luke's.

Ellie vaguely remembered Luke had a younger brother but old Mrs Farrell had hated Ellie so much, Ellie hadn't spent much time at the Farrell house. She shrugged. It was all history.

Belinda Farrell was only five years younger than Ellie, but when she walked in, she looked more eighteen than the twenty-two the computer said she was. And Belinda wasn't happy about seeing Ellie.

It was a shame, because Ellie loved Belinda's tiny silver crocodile that hung from the hoop in her belly button, so they had something in common. Below Belinda's rounded abdomen, the little crocodile's ruby-chip eyes seemed to wink.

But Belinda scowled. 'I'm fine. Why can't I just see Luke and get out of here?' She sat reluctantly in the chair in Ellie's tiny room and crossed her arms over her stomach.

Ellie sat on the other chair and glanced pointedly out the door to the reception room. 'There's still another lady in front of you, so why don't I take your blood pressure and weigh you now? I can write it on your card and then you'll be quicker out when Luke is ready for you.'

Belinda shrugged and uncrossed one arm to allow Ellie to wrap the black cuff around her upper arm.

Ellie glanced across at the young woman's face. 'So, how have you been feeling since you last came and saw Luke?' Ellie noted that Belinda's blood pressure was slightly elevated and her ankles mildly swollen. Hypertensive disease of pregnancy was most common in young first-time mothers.

'Fine!' The young woman dared Ellie to say different and Ellie bit her lip as she looked away.

She finished her observations and tried again. 'Have you thought much about your labour?'

'Nope. I'm not worried.' This time Belinda avoided Ellie's eyes and the answer was less emphatic.

'That's great.' Ellie took the yellow antenatal card to record the blood pressure on and then stood up to pull out the scales for Belinda to stand on. The card showed that Belinda hadn't been for a visit for nearly five weeks. What was Luke doing? That wasn't good enough, especially at Belinda's late stage of pregnancy.

She carried on conversationally, 'When I was due to have my baby, I was a bit nervous. Have you managed to attend antenatal classes at all? Or do any reading about labour?'

'No. I didn't want to go to classes on my own! And I haven't read the book thing that Luke gave me. It's too big. Can I go now?' Belinda remained standing after she'd stepped off the scales.

'Sure. You can sit back out in the waiting room or I could grab some quick stuff to read about labour off the internet if you like—just while you're waiting for Luke to finish with the lady in front of you.'

The girl hesitated and then sat down. 'That would be OK.'

Ellie almost sighed with relief. There was something really strange going on here but she tried to figure out how she could help Belinda the most. Ellie's fingers flew over the keyboard as she searched the Web for her favourite pages on birth and birth education. She looked for one with lots of pictures and very little medical jargon.

Ellie glanced over her shoulder. 'So who's going to be with you when you have your baby?'

When Belinda shrugged, Ellie pressed the 'print' key for the pages she'd found and turned back properly to face the young woman.

'What about your partner or your mother?' Ellie firmly believed in the advantages of a caring support person for a labouring woman.

'My husband is dead. So is my mother. Didn't Luke tell you?' Belinda shrugged. 'Travis was Luke's brother and their mother can't stand me.' Belinda stood up and Ellie quickly grabbed the papers out of the printer and handed them to her. *Déjà vu.* Poor Belinda. The witch strikes again.

'I'm really sorry to hear that. Take these and have a

read. We should have around four weeks before your baby is due so come in a little earlier next week and I'll go through some labour stuff with you.' She looked directly at Belinda. 'My baby's father died before Josh was born, too, and I'd like to help you.'

Belinda stared back and absently rubbed her stomach protectively. 'I might do that.' It wasn't much of an overture but perhaps Belinda had decided she wasn't a threat. Then Luke appeared at her shoulder and any stiffness that had eased in the young woman returned full force as Belinda turned awkwardly away towards his room.

'Hi, Belinda. It's good to see you,' he said. He shot a glance at Ellie as if to say, I hope you did better with her than I usually do. Ellie nodded reassuringly and he turned away to follow his sister-in-law.

Five-thirty arrived out of nowhere. June locked the front door after the last patient and then left—without saying goodnight. Ellie tidied her room and closed down her computer.

'So how was your first day?' Luke appeared at her door and the tiny room shrank to a shoebox. It really wasn't fair for one man to be so attractive and Ellie stamped down a sudden ridiculous urge to lay her head on his chest.

'Sometimes busy—sometimes slow. Very different to working in an obstetric ward but I can see it could be satisfying.' Ellie smoothed her skirt. Luke looked as pristine as he had this morning but she felt a little worse for wear after the hectic day.

'You did well with Belinda,' Luke said. 'She's half promised to come back next week. I've been trying to get her to attend more often, without much success.'

'So I noticed on the card.' Ellie glanced up and her voice gentled. 'How long ago did your brother die?' She hoped he didn't mind talking about his brother but she needed to know.

Luke's face tightened. 'Six months. They'd been married for less than two years when he went for a swim one day and never came back. They never found Travis's body and it's been hard for all of us.'

He met Ellie's eyes. 'I've been worried about Belinda but she shuts everyone out. I thought maybe it was me, and even suggested she go to another doctor, but she didn't turn up there at all. June's been wonderful and rings and reminds her when she doesn't turn up. I don't even know if Belinda really wants this baby.'

Ellie remembered Belinda's hand over her stomach. 'She wants this baby all right. And we'll have to watch her blood pressure.' Luke nodded and Ellie turned away to reach for her handbag.

Luke followed her to the car park and she was more aware of his body next to hers than she should be. She needed to remind herself that Bell's River was for her and Josh as a twosome. Josh deserved his mother's full attention.

Then Luke smiled at her and any wall she'd erected between them melted like butter at his feet.

'You did well for your first day. Goodnight, Ellie.' Luckily he turned away before Ellie could do something dumb like smear herself all over his chest because of a little compliment.

She was a basket case if someone offered her kindness. Look where it had got her with Steve—widowed and terrified of another man dying on her and the grief that entailed.

And Luke was more conservative than poor Steve. He'd want marriage, social obligations and commitment to stay in one place, when all Steve had wanted had been a son to carry on his name before he died.

She jammed her car key into the door lock with unnecessary force and wrenched the key around to escape the memories. She heard Luke start his car and she twisted her key to unjam it, with disastrous results. The door didn't open but the key broke off in the lock with a sickening snap.

Ellie closed her eyes and prayed for Luke to drive out so she could crawl away and call her road service club. No such luck. She heard his engine stop.

'I've never actually seen anybody break the key off in the lock.' Luke's voice came from behind her and there was no use pretending otherwise.

The heat crawled up her neck and into her cheeks as she turned to face him. 'Well, now you have. And before you ask, I don't have another key, but I do have road service insurance.'

'Handy,' was all he said and then he smiled. Suddenly it didn't seem too bad he'd caught her doing something dumb. 'How about I drop you off at the preschool to save you being late. You could phone them from there?'

It would be churlish to refuse the lift but she hesitated. Ellie had an inexplicable fear of Josh becoming as smitten by Luke as everyone else seemed to be. For some reason she couldn't quite explain, she'd hoped she could avoid them meeting. Maybe she still could if she got out of his car fast.

'Thank you. If it's not too far out of your way.'

'Nowhere is too far in Bell's River.' He moved over to his black BMW and opened the passenger door for her. Ellie couldn't remember the last time someone had opened any door for her—it had probably been Luke ten years ago. It was an old-fashioned gesture but made her feel special.

The smell of leather and polish settled over her and she sneaked a look at her shoes to see if they were clean enough to rest on the carpet.

The car rocked gently as Luke climbed in the other side and Ellie stared straight ahead. It was crowded in the front despite the space between the seats. Or it felt crowded anyway, with over six feet of man beside her. He pulled out of the car park smoothly and Ellie realised she hadn't given directions to the school. He seemed to be going the right way.

'So...' Luke didn't take his eyes from the road. 'Today is your son's first full day away from you at the preschool. He'll be glad to see you.'

'I saw him at lunch.' She glanced across at his profile. 'How did you know which preschool to go to?'

He shrugged without looking at her. 'There's only one you could walk to.'

Ellie realised he'd known where she'd gone for her meal break. It was no big deal. She'd just have to get used to living in a small town again.

Moments later he pulled in front of the gaily painted school building and Ellie snatched up her handbag. She quickly opened the door and climbed out. 'We'll be all right from here. Thanks for the lift.'

He turned the engine off. 'I'd like to come in.'

Ellie froze. 'Why?'

'To meet your son.' He tilted his head. 'If that's OK with you?'

So what was she supposed to say? No? She sighed and waited for him to get out of the car. Luke gave her a level look. A look that said, I know you want rid of me, but I'm not going. Ellie felt trapped. She forced herself to relax. It was no big deal. Luke came to stand beside her and Ellie lifted the latch on the childproof gate to find her son.

When Josh saw his mother he clambered to his feet and ran towards her, although he slowed when he noticed Luke standing beside her. Josh was a thin, pale child with Ellie's eyes and her glorious red hair. The boy hesitated for a moment before coming right up to them. Luke could see his determination not to be shy.

Ellie knelt down and cuddled him. 'Hello, darling. This is Dr Farrell, the man I work for.'

'How do you do, Dr Farrell?' Josh held out his hand to shake and Luke took the tiny hand between his fingers.

'Hello, Josh. How was your day?' What else could he say?

'It took a long time.' The little boy shrugged. 'My friends went home at three o'clock and it's mostly just babies here now.'

Ellie hugged him again and then stood up. 'Well, it's time to go home now. I need to use the phone first and then we'll get your bag and say goodbye to the teacher.'

Luke watched her arrange Josh's departure and for the road service to meet her at the preschool. Josh stayed glued to her side the whole time. She probably wasn't aware of Luke's existence and he wasn't even sure why he was there. Except he'd needed to see her son. The reasoning behind that escaped him, too.

Mother and son came back and he could see that Ellie was distracted as they left the preschool grounds.

Luke stopped beside his car. 'If I can't be of any help, I'll go now.' He reached out and shook Josh's hand again. 'Nice to meet you, Josh.'

The little boy was very solemn. 'Bye, Dr Farrell.'

'I'll see you tomorrow, Luke,' Ellie said, and for a

moment he thought she was going to ask him to stay. But she didn't. Luke waved and turned away. The boy was like his mother. He shouldn't have gone in.

Ellie watched him climb into his car. The dumb thing was that she was disappointed he'd left. Thirty seconds later, for some strange reason, the white line down the middle of the road looked wavy.

With a start, she realised she'd been holding her breath until his car had turned the corner. She shook her head. This was ridiculous.

Tuesday morning flew past in a blur of clients, and apart from an enquiry about the lock on her car door, Ellie didn't see much of Luke. He had a visit from one of the pharmaceutical company representatives during his lunch-break and Ellie went off to Josh's preschool. Her son had been a little clingy that morning and Ellie was glad she was only working three days a week.

Back at the surgery, Luke waited for her to put her bag away and then gestured her into his room before the afternoon appointments started.

Ellie sat down in the client's chair and Luke prowled around the room. Now what had she done? Ellie chewed her lip and watched him uneasily.

He stopped in front of her and laced his hands. 'I need to clarify a couple of areas in which we may conflict with our suggestions for labour.'

Mavis Donahue, Ellie thought, and sat forward in her chair, prepared to fight.

'Mrs Donahue...' He paused and nodded when Ellie nodded. 'She came in this morning and she's booked for her second Caesarean birth under general anaesthetic next week. She tells me that she's changed her mind and now she'd like the opportunity for a trial of normal labour or an epidural Caesarean if necessary.'

He paced the room. 'While I have no problem with such a birth plan in this sort of scenario, you weren't here for her last birth. The poor woman went through the mill before we performed a Caesarean delivery on her. I assumed she was horrified at the thought of going through that experience again and was very happy that her labour would be more civilised this time.' He sent her a hard stare but Ellie refused to drop her eyes. She waited to see whether he was going to say more and when he didn't she stopped swinging her leg.

'Well, she's not,' Ellie said flatly. 'While Mavis hopes the labour and the delivery will end in a natural birth, we have discussed an epidural Caesarean scenario so that she can be awake in Theatre when the baby is born. And have her husband by her side if it happens.'

'She didn't tell me that.' Luke shot a look at her. 'I'm sorry, Ellie, but I am a little concerned that this is all your idea and not hers. When I asked her last week if she had any questions, she said no.'

Ellie met his eyes sympathetically and sat back. He genuinely hadn't known his client had felt that way. It was Ellie's job to educate him. 'You should know that when a woman says no—or yes for that matter—she doesn't always mean it.'

His lips thinned and suddenly the room filled with undercurrents neither of them wanted to explore. The hairs stood up on her arms at the brief flare of emotion in his eyes, and she wished she could have told him it hadn't been her fault she hadn't come back, but that would be too personal. She rubbed her arms and ignored the temptation.

Ellie hurried on, 'Anyway, I gave Mavis the information and asked her about her last labour, and she said it had been pretty bad. She also said she'd been very down after that experience.' Luke nodded so Ellie continued.

'Mavis says she had difficulty feeling close to her daughter. She believes that it is because with a general anaesthetic she didn't really wake up until baby was several hours old. It had been more like a surgical procedure than having a baby, and she didn't feel like her child's mother for months after.'

Ellie's voice dropped. 'That frightened her...' she met Luke's eyes '...and she doesn't want that to happen again, so we talked about her being conscious. Then she said she actually felt like a failure because she hadn't been able to deliver her baby vaginally.'

Luke snorted and sat down behind his desk to glare at Ellie. 'Of course she's not a failure. That's the most ridiculous thing I've ever heard.'

Ellie narrowed her own eyes and then shook her head decisively. 'It's a very common perception held by women who have unexpected Caesareans. Unfortunately, only a very few of these women discuss with their doctor the options for subsequent births. And even fewer obstetricians give them encouragement to do so.' She looked at him. 'The majority of women will do whatever their obstetrician recommends without discussion. Surely you know that?'

He shrugged uncomfortably. 'In Mavis's case I saw how distressed she became in labour and I didn't think she would want to go through that again. Her husband certainly asked me not to let it happen again.'

'It's Mavis's choice—no one else should make that for her—and every baby and every labour is different.' Ellie's eyes shone. 'The whole concept of birth is mystical. When a baby decides the time is right, and when the mother's body agrees and the first signs of labour appear, these are special moments. The lead-up to established labour and the mechanisms of spontaneous delivery should be given as much leeway as possible. Intervention is still available if needed but give nature a go first if the mother wants it.'

'But does she?' He was unconvinced and the hardness in his voice told Ellie he believed Mavis's change of birth plan was Ellie's fault.

'Yes.' Ellie was adamant. 'Mavis just didn't know she had a choice and I think that's unenlightened in this day and age.'

Luke poked a finger in Ellie's direction. 'And what if she works herself up to a natural birth and it doesn't happen? Don't you think you've set her up to feel a failure one more time?'

Ellie shook her head vehemently. 'No. Because we've made a birth plan that includes that contingency, and Mavis now has control over that part of her labour, too.'

He ran his hand through his hair in exasperation. 'Like what?'

Ellie shrugged. 'It's only the little things but they are very important for the birthing woman.' Ellie ticked them off on her fingers. 'Epidural, not general anaesthetic. Background music, even to the precise song at birth to always be associated with that special moment. A camera or maybe even video as baby is held by his or her parents for the first time and a blanket on information until Mum knows the baby's weight, which won't happen until Mum is back on the ward.'

Luke drummed his fingers on the desk. 'So she believes she'll cope with a Caesarean if the natural labour doesn't work out?'

Ellie nodded. 'Better than she would if she had another Caesarean under general anaesthetic and not even try for a natural birth.' Ellie grinned. 'But I reckon she'll have the baby vaginally. The last one was much bigger by all accounts and she spent most of her labour on the bed. This time she's going for an active labour.'

Luke closed his eyes for a second before he stood up to walk towards the door. He held it open for her. 'Spare me the eternal optimism of a midwife.'

Ellie walked past and grinned, and Luke restrained the urge to pull her back into the room. Not to discuss Mavis Donahue but to find out all the things he wanted to know about the last ten years. But he wouldn't do that. It wasn't his style. Maybe it should have been.

CHAPTER THREE

LUKE went back into his room without calling the next patient through. Then he opened and closed his fingers to relax the tension in them—and to stop himself from hitting something. Two days with Ellie and he was going mad.

What the hell had happened to the life he'd envisioned when he'd been twenty-two?

Sure, he'd studied hard in med school, instead of following Ellie around, because he'd always planned to take over his father's practice. That five-year pact to meet Ellie again should have tied everything together neatly when they'd both done what they'd needed to do.

Then that horrific night his mother had told him that Ellie wasn't coming back to him he'd realised he should have searched her out earlier. That she was the other half of his dreams—but it had been too late.

Much to his mother's dismay, Luke had chosen England to study obstetrics because Australia was too full of memories of Ellie, and he needed to make a life without her. He'd returned only twelve months ago, just before his father had died. Luke had come back to take over the family practice and had been determined to find a real partner—not a dream—to share his life with. But even that had been a disaster.

With his father and Travis both dying so closely together in time, he'd barely had a moment to think of himself, let alone marriage.

Finally, he'd decided he'd waited long enough to restart his life and Anthea had seemed the perfect answer. She would be a good wife. She was calm, and always perfectly groomed. She understood his profession as a midwife herself and his mother adored her.

So last week he had asked Anthea to marry him and she'd said yes.

Luke massaged his temples. He had no plans to throw away a strong and stable relationship because he lusted after a woman who had already proved unreliable once. But Ellie's return was lousy timing. Maybe she'd would only stay for a few months—just enough to complicate his life again if he let her—and move on.

He should do the sensible thing—stay clear of Ellie and her son, and marry Anthea as he'd planned. Either way, he needed to talk to Anthea because she didn't deserve even internal disloyalty.

He squared his shoulders and walked towards the door and his next patient. He'd ring Anthea and invite himself to tea tonight. He'd try to explain, but he wasn't looking forward to it. He should never have hired Ellie.

Luke knocked on Anthea's door at exactly seven p.m. When she answered the door she looked immaculate, as she always did. In fact, he couldn't remember seeing her anything but. Which meant they'd both done very little together that required strenuous activity. He shook his head. This was his future wife!

'Hello, Luke. Come in.' She stood back to allow him to enter and kiss her cheek as he went past. Then he stopped. She looked up, surprised, as Luke captured her hand and raised it to his lips.

'Come here, Anthea.' He pulled her closer to him and her eyes widened as drew her into his arms. When he kissed her she stiffened, although he could tell she was trying to relax. He lingered for a moment and then let her go.

'I'm sorry, Anthea. That wasn't fair.' He gestured for her to precede him into the dining room and then followed her through. They sat at their usual places and he poured the light beer she'd put out for him and a juice for her.

He went on as if compelled to. 'I just realised we'd never seen each other anything but in control.'

The glass of juice froze on the way to her lips. 'You're acting very strangely, Luke. Is anything the matter?'

'No. Not precisely.' He smiled wryly at her startled expression. 'Do you remember when I asked you if you'd ever been in love and you said we didn't need to discuss that?'

She frowned and then nodded. 'So?'

'And I told you I was once in love when I was very young, but things didn't work out between us?'

She nodded again but this time her face was without expression.

'That woman was Ellie, my new practice nurse.' He met her eyes. 'I won't lie to you. I'm finding it difficult to ignore her even though I realise that my future lies with you.'

She looked down into her glass for a moment and then lifted her eyes again to his. 'Thank you for telling me.' Her lips twisted wryly. 'I think.' She paused. 'So the kiss tonight was what?'

He shrugged. 'Me telling myself that you are the woman that I'm going to marry.'

She raised her dark eyebrows and he wished for the first time she wouldn't wear so much make-up. 'In that case, I'm glad you kissed me. If you need more reassurance, you know where I live.' She lifted the lid on the casserole. 'Perhaps we should eat before this goes cold.'

Luke's lips twitched. He could rely on Anthea. But had he really resolved anything?

On Wednesday morning, Luke was called away to the maternity ward for an emergency Caesarean birth just after ten a.m. So it was just Ellie and June. Ellie saw any of the women who arrived before June could reschedule their appointments for later in the day.

One of Luke's clients didn't have an appointment but had come anyway. Mrs Hollows was thirty-five and this was her first baby.

'We'll have to reschedule your appointment, Mrs Hollows, but in the meantime, I'm Ellie, Dr Farrell's midwife.'

'Hello, Ellie, I'm Louise.' The blonde woman smiled and sat down on the chair in Ellie's room. 'He's a dish, isn't he?' Ellie blinked but didn't need to search for words because Louise was happy to keep talking. 'Luke was the most eligible bachelor in town until Anthea Roberts struck gold. Lucky woman. Anyway, I shouldn't gossip, and I'm not due for a real appointment today. I've come because I do have a couple of questions to ask Luke and he said to come in any time I was worried.'

Ellie smiled encouragingly. 'So you should. Maybe I can help. I'll try, anyway.'

Louise looked a little shamefaced. 'It's taken my husband and I ten years to fall pregnant with this baby, though it feels like for ever. Now that we've actually passed the thirty-week stage, I guess I'm stressing that everything is going to be all right.'

Ellie remembered her own pregnancy. 'It's usual for a first-time mum and even a fifth-time mum to feel that way. You said you had a couple of questions. It's your job as a mother to find out about things that worry you in your pregnancy. That's why I'm here.'

As far as Ellie was concerned, Louise wanting to ask questions was perfectly normal. 'So are you feeling the baby move?'

A beatific smile spread across Louise's face. 'Oh, yes, especially when I'm in bed. Baby kicks quite hard sometimes and my husband has even felt her kick in bed at night.' She looked up confidingly. 'We had an amniocentesis so we know it's a girl.' She shrugged and went on. 'One of the things I worry about is that she doesn't seem to kick as much through the day.'

Ellie nodded. 'People usually feel their baby is more active at night because during the day they're busier and distracted by people and noise and other activities. At night, when you finally stop moving and the lights are out, you notice the baby's movements more. If you slowed down your activity in the day and rested more, you would feel more movements. Does your baby have a special awake time when you notice her most?'

Louise laughed. 'Two a.m. She often wakes me then. I hope that doesn't mean she's a night owl.'

'I've found that the routines babies establish in the womb are often carried over after they're born.' Ellie smiled. 'I'm betting baby has a two a.m. feed in mind when you take her home from the hospital.'

'I wouldn't care if she did,' Louise said. 'I just can't wait until I can hold my baby. And then I would be able to see that she's all right.' She looked across at Ellie and bit her lip. 'I know this sounds stupid, but last night I dreamt my baby wasn't normal.'

Ellie nodded. 'It's not stupid at all. It's horrible when that happens. I remember before my son was born, I dreamt he had no hands. It was really strange and upset me for days because I couldn't tell him that it was OK and as his mother I'd love him anyway.' She grinned. 'Of course, when he was born he did have hands but I must admit that was the first thing I looked for.'

'So it's normal to have a scary dream like that?' Louise looked hopefully at Ellie, who nodded.

'It's more common than you imagine. And there are other types of dreams you can have, too.' Ellie grinned. 'Especially towards the end of your pregnancy when your libido can have a surge that takes your husband by surprise.'

Louise blushed. 'It's funny you should say that. I wasn't going to ask Luke about that—he and my husband are good friends—but I can ask you.' She lowered her voice. 'Is it dangerous to make love this far into the pregnancy? I was beginning to think that my husband didn't find me attractive. Then he said he was scared he might hurt the baby if we made love. That's not true. Is it?'

Ellie shook her head. 'But again that's a normal reaction to a first pregnancy and especially such a precious one as this.' She leaned across and whispered in Louise's ear. 'Men worry they're going to poke the baby in the head.'

'That's what he said.' They both laughed and Ellie could tell Louise was relieved to have discussed it. But there was some care to be taken.

'Have you had any bleeding in this pregnancy?'

Louise nodded. 'At eight and twelve weeks I had a little spotting.' She shuddered. 'We actually thought we'd lose the baby then.'

'It's the most common time for miscarriage.' Ellie rested her hand on lightly on Louise's knee for a second in sympathy for what must have been a worrying time.

She couldn't imagine her life without Josh in it. 'For some women it's normal to spot some blood at the time their usual period would be due if they weren't pregnant. That's how some women don't realise they are pregnant until quite late in their pregnancy. They think they're having a lighter period so can't be pregnant.'

But the conversation did beg the question. Ellie bit her lip. 'Does that mean you haven't made love all pregnancy?' Louise shook her head forlornly and Ellie smiled. 'So how's your husband?'

'Anguished.' They both laughed. 'And to tell you the truth, so am I. I miss that special closeness.'

Ellie gave Louise a direct look. 'As long as making gentle love isn't painful for you, it would be quite safe. Have a play around with positions to find the most comfortable ones.' Both women smiled. 'You may even experience a few tightenings in your tummy afterwards. But unless your doctor has banned it for another reason, there's no reason to avoid making love. Towards the end of pregnancy, it's even good for softening your cervix to prepare you for labour. But at this stage of pregnancy your body won't let that happen.'

Louise's eyes sparkled and she stood up. 'Thank you, Ellie. I really enjoyed talking to you and I do feel much better now.'

'That's great, Louise. Remember you can ring me, too.

'I will. Say hello to Luke for me. Lucky you to work with him.' She grinned wickedly. 'I'll be in to see him next week for my usual appointment.'

Just as they moved into the empty waiting room, Luke pushed open the door from the car park and smiled at them both.

'I see you've met Ellie,' he said. Louise grinned back as she searched blindly for her car keys in her bag.

'I have. Now, don't lose her because I love her already.' She held up her keyring in satisfaction and waved to them both. 'See you Monday.'

'Bye,' Luke and Ellie chorused, and then the door shut behind her. Because June hadn't expected him back so early, there were no more patients scheduled until after lunch. June was in the kitchen, washing up as Ellie had made them both coffee as a peace offering. Luke and Ellie were alone and an awkward silence settled over them before Luke turned towards his room and beckoned Ellie to follow him.

'So tell me what Louise wanted, and who else came in while I was out.' He spoke over his shoulder as he slipped his keys into his desk drawer.

'We've been discussing sex.' Ellie's voice held a hint of mischief and then she reeled off the names of three other women who had been to see her while he'd been out.

Luke turned back to face her. 'Really?'

'Really what?' Ellie sat down in his client's chair and crossed her legs. She saw Luke follow the movement of her ankles and her stomach tightened. He wasn't immune to her and morally she shouldn't be glad about that—but she was. She dragged her mind back to the conversation. 'Who were the women? Or was I really discussing sex with your patient?'

One foot swung back then forward, and he realised why her stockings matched her skin. She wasn't wearing any.

Then she sent his brain reeling again. 'You always were a gentleman, Luke. Too much so.' An unspoken memory hung in the air between them for a moment before she went on. 'But you need to make sure your women know they can make love during their pregnancy.'

Maybe if he hadn't been a gentleman all those years ago, everything might have turned out differently. He closed his eyes for a second and deliberately controlled his impulse to pull Ellie into his arms and kiss the mischief away from those teasing lips of hers.

Having her here was a bad idea all round. But he hadn't felt so alive in years. He tried to picture Anthea and he could see the outline of her but her face wouldn't come into focus. Suddenly life was more complicated than he'd intended and it was all Ellie's fault.

'Have I met the woman who had the Caesarean today?' Ellie's voice brought him back to the present and he grasped the change of subject with relief. He visualised the pale face of the woman he'd operated on.

'No. Sally Carter was thirty-seven weeks pregnant with a sudden retro-placental bleed.'

He sat on the corner of the desk. 'Her husband fell off his motorbike in front of her. She panicked and lifted the bike off him in a surge of adrenaline.' He shook his head at the wonders a body could perform in an emergency. 'She's only a little woman. Luckily they live in town and when she felt the pain straight after, the ambulance brought her in, too.'

All humour was gone from Ellie's face. 'And the baby?'

'He's had a rough morning and is still a couple of weeks early, but I'd say he'll be fine. I was going to ship him out to the base hospital, but if we can keep up the staffing for a midwife to stay with him in the nursery, then he can remain with his mum. Sally's pretty blown away by it all.'

'I'll bet. We had a little one last year in Sydney who

died when the placenta separated prematurely from the wall of the uterus. Everyone was devastated. What about Sally's husband?'

'Bill's fine. Cracked a couple of ribs and burnt his ankle where the bike trapped him, but well enough to sit with his wife and stare at their son.' Luke remembered the awe on Bill's face at his child's tiny hands and feet. 'It could all have ended tragically, but I'd lay odds that some of Bill's immaturity was knocked out of him today.' He stood up.

'I'm off to lunch—do you want to join me? We can have an extra half-hour and you'll still have time to visit Josh's school.' He regretted the invitation as soon as he'd offered it. For his own peace of mind, he needed less time with his practice nurse, not more. But there were things he had to find out.

Ellie uncrossed her legs and stood up. 'Sounds good. Can we still go next door if I don't have a burger?' He dragged his eyes away from her smile and nodded.

Luke watched Ellie crunch her way though the plate of fries she'd ordered, and when she licked the salt from her fingers it brought back memories of other nights they'd had take-aways down at the cove. Other nights he'd suggested a restaurant and she'd preferred just the two of them. He said the first thing that came into his head to get his mind away from the past.

'So, are you planning to settle down in Bell's River or move on, like your mother, when the time comes?' It had all the subtlety of a sledgehammer but was probably the biggest question he had and his best chance for staying faithful to Anthea.

Her gaze lifted to his. 'I'm not my mother, Luke.' She brushed her hands together to get rid of the last of the salt. 'Are you asking me as my employer or because we were once friends?'

He couldn't believe she could be so laid-back about their past.

He leaned across the table towards her. His fingers tightened as he crumpled the empty can of soda in his hand. His voice was low and the tinge of sarcasm wasn't like him. 'We were more than friends—I asked you to marry me!' She sat back in her chair and he dropped the can on its side and sat back in the chair himself. 'But that's beside the point.'

She frowned and shook her head. 'That was a long time ago. I may be presumptuous here, Luke, but I need to state that I'm not looking for a relationship. Josh is my life. And you're engaged.'

'Thank you for reminding me,' he said dryly. 'I wasn't asking for an affair, my life is too complicated for that, I was asking if you can see yourself living here for ever.'

'Why do you need to know?' she said.

He watched her bite her lip and when he didn't answer, couldn't answer, he saw her shrug.

When she said, 'I don't think so,' he didn't know whether to be relieved or devastated.

She looked away. 'It's harder than I thought to come back to somewhere you have memories.'

Luke felt a fierce anger pierce his gut at her admission and his voice hardened again. 'So you do have good memories from here?'

She glared at him impatiently. 'Cut me a break, Luke. I was barely seventeen when I left. You were this god who not only deigned to talk to me but treated me like a princess. We fell in lust and had some fabulous times. Then I moved on.' She looked away.

His voice dropped. 'You promised you would come back in five years. And you didn't come back.'

She refused to meet his eyes. 'There were reasons and I don't think anything I say will change that. I'd rather not discuss it.'

'Fine. Let's not discuss it. Tell me about your husband.'

He didn't know why he was putting himself through this unless he thought he'd be able to walk away more easily if he could understand why she hadn't come back.

He watched her face soften and jealousy surged up where it had no right to be.

'Steve was a good man.' She turned the silver ring on her left hand. 'We went to uni together to do our nursing and became very close. When I was married to him it was like living with my best friend. Both his parents had died and the saddest thing was that he wasn't alive to see the son he'd wanted so badly.'

Luke was sorry he'd asked. He didn't know what he'd expected to hear, but it wasn't marital bliss. Served him right.

Ellie pushed her plate away. 'So what have you been doing for the last ten years?' Her question caught him off guard. He wasn't the only one who wanted answers.

He laughed, and the sound almost stuck in his throat. You mean after I found out you were never coming back to me? He didn't say it. 'I went to England for O and G and came back here just over a year ago to help my father in the practice. He was sick and I should have come back sooner. Dad died and then Travis went missing a few months later.' He looked away from the sympathy in her eyes. 'It's been hard for my mother and I've tried to be there for her. One day I woke up and realised I was thirty-two years old and didn't have any life except for my work. That was when I started going out with Anthea.'

'So, tell me about Anthea.' Her voice was almost too bright.

He couldn't see himself calmly discussing Anthea with Ellie. 'I don't think so. I'm sure you'll meet her at the surgery one day when she drops in to visit me.'

Ellie stood up and he watched her take the money for her lunch from her purse and put it on the table in front of him. She gave that half-wave but didn't say anything as she walked away and he stared after her. The worst of it was he was just as besotted by her as he'd been ten years ago. But the attraction was definitely one way— she had moved on. He'd be better to forget the past. She obviously had.

Ellie's feet tapped on the pavement as she walked. She didn't really want to know how Luke had fallen in love with his fiancée anyway. What she needed to know was how her son was going at school today. The conversation had given her indigestion and she'd do well to remember that if he asked her to lunch again.

Back at the surgery, the afternoon list was a nightmare. Patients were banked back to the door to see Luke, and Ellie couldn't see how the clinic could finish much before six o'clock. Which was a nuisance, because the hospital had rung and asked her to do a night duty that night and the next and she needed to arrange for Josh to stay over at the Judds'.

Finally the waiting room was empty. The last patient for the day was Summer Brown. Summer was expecting twins in three weeks, and even with that time to go, Ellie winced when she saw how big the young woman's stomach was.

'Hi, Summer. I'm Ellie, the midwife. How're you feeling?'

Summer pushed a strand of blonde hair off her forehead in a tired gesture. 'Exhausted. And I'm dreading the next few weeks.' She sank into the chair and held out her arm for Ellie to take her blood pressure.

Ellie smiled at Summer's obvious experience with antenatal visits. 'I see on your card you've two other pre-schoolers at home. Have you someone to help you through the day?'

'Not through the day, but at night, after he's finished work, my husband is wonderful. So I put my feet up most of the evening.'

Ellie whistled sympathetically. 'Have you thought about contacting a community group like Grannies Anonymous?'

Summer shook her head and her bemused look encouraged Ellie to explain. 'It's a free service and not means-tested. The group is made up of older ladies whose children have grown up and they have some spare time on their hands. A co-ordinator matches them to a family just to give you someone to help with the children. They don't do cleaning or housework, but will amuse the other children if you need a lie-down in the afternoon or want them to take the little ones to the park.'

'Are you sure we have a group like that in Bell's River? It sounds too good to be true.'

'My neighbour is part of one and she was telling me about it. She and her husband are wonderful with my son.'

Summer sighed. 'I'd have to talk to my husband about it but it would be a godsend for the next couple of weeks at the very least.'

Ellie nodded. 'And even after the babies are born,' she said with a grin.

Summer heaved herself to her feet and stepped onto the scales. 'My husband is having a month away from work. Neither of us has any parents and a bit of help might take some of the load off him. This pregnancy was an accident and when we found out we were having twins we didn't know what to do. I'm sure we'll manage but I will talk to him about Grannies.'

Ellie picked up Summer's handbag from the floor to save her having to bend down again. She offered Summer a smily card with her home phone number on it. 'I'll find out who the contact person is from my neighbour. You can ring me at home any time or here after next Monday.'

Summer still looked a little unsure and Ellie gestured with her hands. 'If anyone deserves some help, it's you. If you're interested, I can arrange it.'

They both looked up as Luke came to the door. 'You're the lucky last, Summer. Are you ready to come through?' Luke looked at Ellie, who nodded and handed him Summer's antenatal card.

'I'll see you next week, Summer.'

Summer set off for Luke's room. 'Thanks, Ellie.'

Fifteen minutes later, Ellie scanned her tidy room and closed down the computer. Josh would be wondering where she was.

Summer had gone and June had huffily headed home, unimpressed about working late. At least she'd said goodnight to Ellie this time. Ellie couldn't figure out why anyone would be so miserable. Maybe June had haemorrhoids.

Ellie suppressed a smile. She grabbed her bag and called out as she went to the door, 'See you next week, Luke.'

His voice floated back from his room. 'Can you wait one minute, Ellie?'

Damn. She wasn't in the mood to fight her attraction to Luke. She glanced at her watch. She'd hoped to get Josh settled at the neighbours by seven-thirty and maybe even catch an hour or two's sleep before she had to get ready for the night shift. She didn't start until ten-thirty so another few minutes wouldn't make that much difference except take even more time away from her and Josh.

'Sorry.' Luke appeared beside her. 'Just backing up my computer. I wanted to say the Grannies idea was a stroke of genius.' He was smiling at her like she'd just given him a winning lottery ticket and she couldn't help but smile back. He really did care about his clients. She just hoped his fiancée appreciated him. She blinked. Now, where had that thought come from?

She shied away from trying to figure it out. 'I'm glad. But I've got to go, Luke.'

'Big date, eh?' He was joking.

Ellie widened her eyes. 'I expect to be up all night.' The smile fell off Luke's face and Ellie grinned as she lifted the latch on the door. 'Bye.'

His 'Be Careful, Ellie' followed her out the door. Luke watched her walk away and it was like she was leaving all over again. Which was ridiculous.

She was a free agent—unlike him—but it was still a shock that she had a new man already and she'd been in town less than two weeks. What did he really know about her anyway? Luke turned back to his room. He'd catch up on some paperwork before he went home. Suddenly he wasn't as hungry as he'd been ten minutes ago.

CHAPTER FOUR

ELLIE stood on the maternity ward verandah and waited for someone to answer the night bell. The cool sea breeze brushed her cheeks and the stars were brighter than she'd ever seen them. She'd lived in so many different towns and cities, and seen a lot of stars, that was saying something.

She wondered where her mother was. The last Ellie had heard, she was working as a masseuse at a health farm in northern NSW. Josh didn't get to see his only grandparent much and Ellie suppressed a twinge of disappointment that her mother didn't visit them more.

Ellie stared at the Milky Way as it frosted thickly in a white sweep across the southern sky, and her thoughts turned to Steve. Since she'd been in Bell's River, he'd been further from her thoughts than she felt comfortable with. She and Josh had picked out a star near the Southern Cross to be his father's star, and Ellie searched for it now.

Steve would have liked it in Bell's River. Ellie breathed deeply and squared her shoulders. She and Josh could have fun together here if she could stop the intrusion of Luke Farrell into her thoughts.

From her previous visit to ask about work, Ellie knew that the maternity ward at Bell's River was small but efficient. They had about three hundred births a year, mostly under the care of Luke and another three general practitioners with obstetric qualifications. But as the only obstetrician, Luke was involved with most emergency cases and any pregnancies that were complicated by pre-existing disease in the mother or high obstetric risk.

The door opened and she turned back to reality. 'Hi. I'm Ellie Diamond, and I'm filling in tonight.'

A tall, freckle-faced woman smiled and stood back to invite her in. 'I'm Sam. Welcome. The supervisor left a uniform in the change room for you.' Ellie liked Sam from the first moment she saw her.

The two evening maternity staff were friendly and seemed glad to know there was another experienced midwife in town to call on for emergencies. The other night midwife that Ellie would share the shift with hadn't arrived yet.

'I'll take you for a quick tour before Anthea comes.' Sam didn't notice that Ellie froze for a moment at that news, and continued down the corridor. 'Then at least you'll have a vague idea where things live if the night gets hectic.'

Ellie nodded. 'I'd like that,' she said, and followed Sam down the carpeted hall. This looked like a great place to work except that Luke's fiancée had to be the person she would be working with. But there wasn't any reason that should be a problem, Ellie decided firmly.

The unit was small but modern and the two birthing rooms seemed more like motel suites than a hospital labour ward. All the emergency equipment was tucked away behind flip-down cupboard doors.

'Very nice.' Ellie's eyes sparkled as she noticed the birth ball for use in the shower for backache relief and the low stool the women could use instead of the bed to give birth.

'I could have a baby here,' Ellie commented, and Sam smiled.

'I've had three and it's the best. But, then, I had good labours.'

Ellie was interested in Sam's thoughts from the mother's point of view. 'So who was your doctor?'

Sam laughed. 'Most of the midwives go to Luke Farrell. Not because he's the only obstetrician—all the GPs are great with their women at birth—but because he's such a sweetie.'

Ellie could imagine Luke would be a calming face to see in labour when you thought it would never end. They walked back towards the desk. 'I've just started work at his rooms this week.'

Sam nodded. 'I thought it would be you.' She grinned. 'Not many new midwives in town.' Ellie grinned back.

'He'd be a delight to work for. He could have any of us except we're all full time here.' The doorbell rang and Sam looked ahead as Julie came from the nursery to open the door. 'We'd better go for report. Anthea Roberts likes to start and finish on time, and as she does the rosters I don't like to get on the wrong side of her,' Sam warned with a smile. 'Not that she isn't fair—because she is.' Sam stopped again and her voice lowered. 'By the way, she and Luke are an item.'

Don't I know it, Ellie thought. She couldn't deny her morbid interest in seeing the woman Luke had chosen. Ellie looked ahead to the sister's station. Anthea Roberts sat straight in her chair like a statue of Cleopatra. Black blow-dried hair and eyeliner at ten-thirty at night seemed a little labour-intensive to Ellie, but she certainly looked a million dollars. Even Ellie could see the stark contrast between herself and Anthea. Each to their own, she thought as she sat down beside the senior sister, but she couldn't help pulling her uniform hem down over her knees to hide the fact that she wore no stockings.

Sam introduced them. 'Have you met Ellie Diamond, Anthea? She's our new casual, and as she works for Luke I wondered if you'd caught up with each other yet.'

Ellie said, 'Hi. Nice to meet you, Anthea.'

Anthea smiled without showing her teeth. 'Hello. Ellie, is it?' She raised one eyebrow delicately. 'Not your proper name, I'm sure.'

'It's the one I use. But don't worry, I won't call you Anthie.'

Sam had a sudden fit of coughing and Anthea frowned as if she didn't understand the answer. Ellie mentally kicked herself and looked helplessly at Sam. Her new friend responded heroically and turned the patient board towards them.

'OK. Better start. We had three discharges today so we only have two inpatients, two nursery babies and one woman in labour.' She grinned at them. 'But that will keep the two of you busy enough.'

Sam caught Anthea's glance at the clock and spoke more quickly. 'In room one we have Sally Carter, today's Caesarean section after an antepartum haemorrhage. She came back from Theatre at twelve-thirty and has an IV line and catheter, and her wound is intact with minimal ooze. She's had pain relief as charted, last given at ten tonight, and hasn't breastfed her baby yet because he was too sick, but she's dying to try.' Sam looked at Ellie and Ellie nodded. Her first job after report.

'As for Baby Carter, he was happily floating around in his mummy's tummy at thirty-seven weeks' gestation when his holiday was interrupted by the placental separation.

'You probably already know this from Dr Farrell, Ellie, but I'll fill you in, Anthea. His silly father dropped a motorbike on his leg and was making toast with the exhaust pipe until Mum lifted it off him. Luckily, young Mr Carter was born within half an hour of the incident so lives to tell the tale.

'His Apgars at birth were two at one minute, three at five minutes and six at ten minutes. He's one lucky little boy and has just been weaned out of the head box oxygen. He's almost recovered enough to have a feed, although his drip will remain *in situ* until Dr Farrell reassesses him in the morning, so he's not ravenously hungry.'

Ellie was hugely enjoying Sam's version of events until she glanced across at Anthea's lemon-lipped expression. Then she sighed. It was going to be a long night. What a shame she wasn't on with Sam.

Sam continued, oblivious to Anthea's lack of humour. 'In room two we have the delightful Mrs Tiang Evans, who had a Caesarean section four days ago for cephalopelvic disproportion. Tiang's managing baby beautifully, her breasts are filling and she manages to attach baby without assistance for his feeds. Her wound is clean and dry and her husband thinks she's the cleverest woman in the world.

'Baby is quite jaundiced and his serum bilirubin was three hundred and twenty. Needless to say, he's in the crib under phototherapy lights but is still feeding well. He's been wet and dirty this shift and had his first bath by Dad today.

'Tiang wants to go home tomorrow if baby's SBR is down enough, but we're trying to persuade her to stay for another couple of days so that she doesn't do too much too soon.'

Anthea nudged Ellie. 'You'll have the nursery.'

Obviously Anthea needed to state her seniority, Ellie

thought, but she refused to let the woman annoy her. Ellie smiled. 'I love the nursery.'

Sam looked at the two of them as if sensing undercurrents then went on. 'In birthing unit two, we have Judy Craig. She's at term, third pregnancy, two previous spontaneous vaginal deliveries here in the last three years. Her waters broke at home at five this afternoon and she came in contracting strongly about an hour ago. She's six centimetres dilated and using the nitrous oxide well for pain relief. Dr Farrell is on call and aware of her admission.'

Sam sat back. 'And that's it.' She handed the keys over to Anthea, caught Ellie's eye and they both stood up.

'If you want to come into the nursery and relieve Julie, you can take over and we'll head home.'

'Sounds good.' Ellie glanced at Cleopatra. 'Let me know if there's anything I can do for you, Anthea.' Anthea inclined her head and Ellie followed Sam into the special care nursery.

Sam suppressed a grin. 'She's not a barrel of laughs, but good on the administrative side and efficient in the labour ward. Anthea likes to decide where she'll work and you won't see much of her while you're stuck in here.' Ellie wasn't too depressed about that.

Sam left Ellie with Julie while she went with Anthea to say goodbye to the labouring woman.

Julie was tall and slim with wavy brown hair. 'Hi, again, Ellie. So you got the nursery.' She gestured around the small nursery with its two humidicribs and one open resuscitaire.

'As you can see, we're a small unit and only keep the stable babies here. If they get too sick we send them off to the base hospital, and if they can't handle them they go to Sydney or Newcastle.' She moved over to the crib with the purple fluorescent lights and patted the roof.

'Our sunbather is in here.' The baby squirmed inside the cot, and Julie slipped her hand in the porthole to adjust the light protective eye covers on his little face. Ellie loved the way a pair of sunglasses had been painted on the blindfold.

'Baby Evans might come out of the crib tomorrow. He's feeding really well and usually that means his bilirubin is falling. We just take him out to Tiang's room for feeds and Mum brings him back when she's finished.'

Julie stepped across to the other crib. 'Mr Carter, whom Dad is considering calling Harley, has been a good boy. Initially his respirations were over eighty but he's settled down to fifty breaths a minute. He's just been graded into room air and his pulse-oximeter is reading ninety-eight per cent so he can go out for his feed soon. The IV has been turned down to four mils an hour because we want him to start thinking about food now.'

She turned back to Ellie. 'The supervisor said you did your neonatal training at North Shore.' Ellie nodded. 'We send our tiniest down to them. I'd like to do my certificate there, too.'

'It's a good unit,' Ellie agreed.

Julie glanced at the clock and grimaced. 'And that's the happy nursery family. I'm on in the morning so I'll see you in less than eight hours. If Anthea needs you in birthing, page the supervisor on 001 and she'll send someone to sit in the nursery while you're busy.'

'Sounds good. Thanks, Julie.'

Julie waved. 'No worries. Most of the time Anthea won't ask for help. She'll call the doctor for the delivery and manage on her own. She doesn't like people...' Julie paused and laughed. 'I should finish that sentence.' She made a show of wiping the smile off her face. 'Anthea doesn't like people looking over her shoulder while she's working, either in the nursery or the labour ward. So she'll ask if she wants you. Have a good night.'

When Julie was gone it was very quiet in the nursery except for the beeping of the heart monitors on both babies. Ellie felt remarkably at home.

The year she'd spent at North Shore Neonatal Intensive Care Unit had shown Ellie what had seemed like every conceivable disease, abnormality and extreme prematurity a baby could suffer. NSH was the receiving hospital from all over the state. Neonatal care wasn't an area Ellie wanted to concentrate on but the experience gained was a great security blanket when things didn't go according to plan in a birth.

The two main realisations Ellie had come away with had been the incredible resilience of babies and their parents, and how much emotional impact a tiny scrap of humanity could have on those around them, including the staff.

Ellie heard the outside door shut as the evening staff went home. Anthea came to the door of the nursery and stared at Ellie without a word.

Ellie raised an eyebrow in enquiry. 'Looking for me?'

Anthea took a step into the room with her eyes not leaving Ellie's face. 'I hear you've done your neonatal and the advanced obstetrics course. Aren't we a little "small fry" for your expertise?'

Ellie smiled easily. 'I love it all.' The sound of a patient call button interrupted and Anthea frowned then turned away with a snap. Ellie tilted her head at the spot where the senior nurse had been. The chance of Anthea becoming a bosom buddy appeared highly unlikely. Which suited Ellie fine.

It would actually have been harder to become friends with Luke's fiancée. As far as Ellie could see, the woman wasn't the warmest person she'd met. But that wasn't Ellie's problem. She was the one who'd told Luke she wasn't interested in a relationship. She meant it. Josh was her first priority and she had no right to care who Luke was engaged to. So why did she? Ellie dragged over a bag of nappies to fold. Busy was good.

Ellie saw little of Anthea for the next two hours as Anthea's patient progressed to imminent delivery.

The outside doorbell rang and Ellie left the nursery to let in the caller. It was Luke.

Ellie stared at him through the glass door. Luke looked like he'd been sitting at home, waiting for the phone. It was one a.m. for heaven's sake. Either that or he slept fully dressed standing up in his wardrobe to arrive looking so well groomed.

His eyes widened and then a slow smile lightened his face when he saw who it was. Ellie pushed open the door and Luke angled himself past her into the ward.

'So this is your all-night hot date,' he said.

Ellie grinned but didn't say anything as she went back to the nursery because she was afraid she'd gush something stupid. Surely she would get used to seeing him at all hours of the day and night. This fizzing excitement when he was in her vicinity was over the top. It was probably just a leftover of that special feeling people said you had for your first real boyfriend.

If he hadn't been engaged, maybe she could have had that one passionate night with him that he'd refused to give her ten years ago?

Just to demystify that feeling of incompleteness she'd carried since then, of course.

It was becoming obvious she should have picked another seaside town to settle with her son if she wanted peace of mind. But she'd thought Luke was safely married. And now that she had seen Luke again, would another town really give her that? She busied herself washing baby bonnets to redirect her thoughts.

After the birth of the Craigs' baby down in the birthing suite, Luke sauntered into the nursery in search of Ellie. She had her back to the door as she soothed an unsettled baby Carter in the crib.

When Luke spoke from behind her, she blinked and focussed her eyes. She realised she was soothing the baby by feel and had been staring unseeingly at the cot.

'Tired?' he said.

Ellie turned slowly to face him and their eyes locked. His were warm and caring and Ellie felt like he'd wrapped his arms around her. Which was a wake-up call. The guy was this sweet to everyone. They were still staring at each other when Anthea came in search of Luke. She looked from one to the other and her lips thinned before she laid her hand on Luke's arm with a proprietorial gesture.

'Come and have a coffee with me before you go home.'

Luke tilted his head towards Ellie and raised his eyebrows. 'If you can't leave the nursery unattended, would you like me to bring you a drink?'

Anthea frowned. 'Ellie can go when I come back. The poor woman *needs* to get out of the nursery some time.' Before Anthea steered Luke away she pointed Ellie down to the birthing unit. 'They're nearly ready to bring baby up for a weigh and a bath. Process it, will you, when they come?' They moved out the door and Ellie could hear Anthea laughing gently with Luke.

Luke allowed himself to be drawn away from Ellie because it was the safest thing to do. He couldn't believe the degree of relief he'd felt when he'd realised she wasn't out for an 'all-nighter' with another man. And he had no right to feel that way. He was engaged to another woman, the woman walking beside him.

Back in the nursery, Ellie shrugged. Cleopatra was a weirdo and she couldn't see what Luke liked about her. Maybe she was conventional, except for the Egyptology, and got on well with Luke's mother. It was Ellie's turn to smile.

Process the baby. 'Sheesh.' Ellie shook her head in disgust as she checked out the paperwork that Julie had left out for her to use after the new baby was born. It sounded like she had to put the baby in one end of a machine and spit it out the other.

She hadn't been asked to assist in the birthing unit and hadn't met the new mother yet. At least the weigh and measure of the baby would take up a little more of the night. This was very different to the hectic nursery nights in the city.

By morning Ellie was weary. That nauseous five a.m. roll of her stomach reminded Ellie how much she hated night duty.

She'd enjoyed meeting Judy and Ray Craig and baby Andrew. At eight pounds he seemed huge compared to the other two in the nursery and when Ellie helped Judy start him at the breast they all laughed at his ferocious expression.

'He's a vacuum-cleaner. You'll have to be very careful with your attachment or he'll damage your nipples.' She grinned at Judy. 'But he's definitely a breast man.' They all laughed and Ellie wrote out a separate piece of paper for Ray to take home with all Andrew's measurements to skite about.

As soon as the shift ended and she'd driven home, Ellie crawled into bed. Mrs Judd was taking Josh with her when she went grocery shopping this morning. Josh loved supermarkets. Ellie would collect him from next door before lunch when she'd had a few hours' sleep.

But it was hard to sleep. Luke was invading her mind and she had to keep telling herself that she'd let Josh down if she became involved Luke. But Ellie was genuinely disturbed about Luke aligning himself with Anthea. The woman was a humourless machine and Luke had the tendency to lean towards precision and predictability as well. Maybe they were suited but Ellie winced at the thought of their poor little boring children. She punched her pillow and tried not to think about Luke having children with another woman. What was the matter with her lately? She needed to relax enough to go off to sleep. It was really none of her business.

When Ellie woke, unrefreshed, it was eleven-thirty and her head felt as woolly as a Merino sheep. She stumbled into the shower and stood under the spray until she started to feel better. By the time she knocked on the Judds' door she was awake even if she felt like curling back up on the bed again.

When Josh saw her he jumped up from the carpet where he was doing a jigsaw and wrapped himself around her legs. 'Hello, my darling.' Ellie mussed his hair and then bent down to hug him.

Lil smiled at them both and suggested a coffee. 'So how was your first shift at the hospital?'

'Good. I saw the unit manager this morning, and she's offered me a permanent Thursday and Friday night duty every week.' Ellie met Lil's eyes. 'I said I'd get back to her tomorrow morning after I'd spoken to you. What do you think? Are you interested in a paid babysitting thing or would you rather I asked someone else?'

Ellie hated how the sleep deprivation of night duty

made her feel but she needed the extra work. And at least on night duty she didn't have to be away during daylight hours. Making ends meet was harder than she'd realised, with Josh's preschool fees and the rent of the house, but if she had a routine, it would get easier. Surely.

'If you'd like to do it, then we're happy to mind Josh for you. But we're not making money out of it.'

Ellie sighed. 'But I'm getting money to do the work.'

'But that's a job. We love having Josh.'

Clem nodded and Ellie racked her brain for a barter solution. She remembered that Lil had mentioned he had a bad back. 'Well, how about I mow your lawn when I do mine, once a week? I'm strong and I enjoy mowing.'

Lil looked at her husband. 'The boy who usually does it has gone away. We'll see.' That was all she'd say.

That night, when Ellie went to work, she was still tired but the ward was busy from the first moment, and she hoped that would carry her through to the morning.

Anthea must have decided that if Ellie loved the nursery, then tonight Ellie would do the labour ward. With that scenario in mind, Ellie tried to look disappointed, but it really was her favourite place. To make it even better, the labouring woman was Summer Brown. Thirty-seven weeks wasn't too early for twins and Summer was well into labour by the time Ellie came on duty.

'Hi, Summer.' Ellie had followed Sam as she went in to say goodnight, and the room seemed full of light and people. To Ellie's mind, Summer looked even more stressed than she should. Ellie's first priority would be to help lessen that waste of energy.

Adam Brown, Summer's husband, held his wife's hand as she breathed through a contraction and two elderly black-cardiganed women Ellie didn't know were sitting on chairs, watching the drama on the bed like crows on a fence.

Summer was facing away from the women and her lips were tight with discomfort and fear. The foetal monitors were strapped to her abdomen with a heart rate being recorded for each twin.

Sam saw the look on Ellie's face and grimaced. 'Dr Farrell wanted frequent traces of the babies' condition so poor old Summer has spent a fair bit of time on the bed.' Ellie just nodded and Sam left to go home.

She looked across at the other women. 'Hi. I'm Ellie. I thought Summer didn't have any relatives from around here.' The younger of the two would have been in her seventies and she smiled at Ellie. 'We're Summer's next-door neighbours and we've come to see the babies born.'

Ellie felt the blood burn between her ears and with great restraint held her peace for the moment. 'That must be exciting for you.' She smiled noncommittally at them and extended her hand towards the door. 'If you would just step outside while I examine Summer for a minute, that would be a great help. I'll see you both shortly.'

The ladies frowned but stood up and went out the door. Ellie followed and shut the door behind them before switching off the main room light so that the lights were dimmer. She crossed over to the bed and perched on the edge beside Summer and started to undo the foetal monitor belts.

'How're you going, Summer? I just want to feel your tummy, if that's all right, and also take your blood pressure—nothing scarier than that.' She looked across at Adam. 'You both seem pretty tense. Did you really want those ladies in here?'

Adam gave a strangled laugh and Summer groaned. 'It was my fault,' she said. 'Adam was at work when I started labour and I couldn't get my phone to work. They brought me in here and now they won't go home.' There was a quiver of tears in her voice.

'I tried to ask them to leave,' Adam said, 'but I didn't like to offend them. Summer might need their help in an emergency one day.'

Ellie smiled. 'Not a problem. I'm an eviction specialist from way back and they'll still talk to you when you get home, I promise.' Adam smiled with relief.

'And as for this monitor...' Ellie glared at the wad of paper that had run through it, 'we have more than enough of this for the time being. We'll do a couple of minutes every hour or so but I'd like to see you spend most of your time in the shower if you can.'

Summer sighed with relief. 'That would be heaven. The hot water seems to help the pain the most.'

Ellie quickly palpated Summer's huge tummy and described the positions the babies were lying in. Both were coming head first and she couldn't see any problems with the birth.

Summer touched Ellie's arm. 'Dr Farrell said I might have to have an epidural, but I really would prefer not to. I didn't have it with my other two.'

Ellie squeezed Summer's leg. 'You don't have to do anything you don't want.' Ellie could see more friendly discussions with Luke coming up. 'Let's move you into the shower so that you're more comfortable.'

By the time Summer was sitting on the blue ball in the shower, even Adam was looking more relaxed.

Satisfied, Ellie placed some towels close by and slipped out of the bathroom.

CHAPTER FIVE

THE phone rang. 'Maternity, Ellie speaking. Can I help you?'

'Ellie?' Luke sounded surprised. 'You there again?'

Ellie frowned at the leap of excitement in her throat. She'd known Summer was Luke's patient so, of course, he was going to ring. She tried for nonchalance. 'Yep. Did you ring about Summer?' Ellie was partially distracted by how she'd get rid of these old ladies before Summer needed her again. 'She's doing really well.'

'How does the CTG seem?' Ellie couldn't help looking across the room at the foetal monitor machine standing alone with the paper dribbling out of it.

'It looks good. Fine. Of course, Summer's in the bathroom, having a shower at the moment, so it's not recording anything.'

Luke's voice lowered dangerously. 'And are you planning on connecting her in the near future?'

Ellie grinned into the phone but realised it was lucky he couldn't see it. 'I thought I'd do a five-minute trace every hour, seeing as there's been enough done to paper a wall already and it's better for her labour if she's off the bed.'

'All right, Ellie. But I'll be looking at the trace as a record of the babies' condition so you'd better have some for me to see when I come in.' She thought he was going to hang up and almost missed his last comment. 'Make sure you give me enough time to be there for the birth or I will not be impressed.'

'Certainly, Doctor,' said Ellie, and put the phone down gently. Luke needed to appreciate how normal labour could be because in Ellie's opinion he seemed to expect things to go wrong too much. But that was the problem with doctors. Still, they were handy people to have around when you needed them.

The elderly ladies were drinking tea in the relatives' waiting room and Ellie had to smile.

'Can we go back in now?' the spokesperson, Rita, said.

'Actually, that's what I came to talk to you about.' Ellie sat down next to them on the long lounge. 'Summer tells me she would have been in big trouble if you hadn't been home.'

Both ladies preened. 'We only did our Christian duty.'

Ellie nodded enthusiastically. 'I'm sure you did. And I think it's amazing that you both are willing to sit here, maybe until the morning, just to make sure Summer is fine.'

Their faces lengthened at Ellie's assumption it would take that long. Ellie went on, 'And most of that time she'll spend in the shower so, of course, I'll have to ask you to wait out here.' She smiled at them both. 'Neither of you look as tired as I thought you would for nearly midnight, so I'm sure you'll be fine.' She glanced around the little room. 'Would you like me to get you both a blanket and some pillows?'

Rita looked across at Gladys. 'My neck is a little sore already from sitting on this lounge. It's a bit of a shame we did promise Summer we'd stay.'

Gladys nodded and Ellie just smiled gently. 'I could mention that you both decided she would be more comfortable in the shower than chatting to you. Do you think she'll believe that?' The ladies looked at each other and nodded, and Ellie stood up.

'When the babies come home, I'm sure Summer will appreciate how close you've all become.'

That really worried them. Ellie tried not to smile as the ladies gathered their things decisively. 'We're not that close to them, you know,' said Gladys uncertainly, 'and I'm not good with babies.'

'Not good with babies,' Rita muttered in agreement, and stood up.

Ellie nodded. 'Sometimes it's hard not to have people expect things from you if you get too close.' The ladies nodded sagely. 'Well, I'll send Summer your best wishes and I'm sure she's very appreciative of your support.'

'Goodnight,' they chorused as they set off towards the exit. Ellie sighed with relief and slipped back into the birthing unit.

Summer spent the next hour in the shower and, judging by her slightly wild-eyed look, was getting close to the transitional stage of labour and almost ready to push. Ellie wanted one more quick trace of the babies' heart rates so they all did a mad dash back to the bed before moving became too hard.

Both babies' heart rates were skipping along merrily and still accelerating when the walls of their mother's uterus tightened around them.

Suddenly Summer exhaled a couple of quick breaths and started to push.

Ellie pressed the nurse's call button for Anthea and quickly dialled Luke's number. He answered straight away. Ellie was brief. 'Summer is in second stage.'

'I'm on my way.' He put the phone down and Ellie turned back to the bed. Anthea came through the door soon after and everything was in readiness for the new arrivals.

By the fourth push a tiny crescent of baby's head had

appeared and Ellie, overgowned and gloved, resigned herself to being in trouble if Luke didn't make it for the first baby's birth.

The door to the unit opened and Luke strode in. Ellie had it all well in hand. There she stood, doing what she loved doing, attuned to the woman and obviously capable. He remembered his first twin delivery and that added sense of excitement and awe he'd felt as he'd been the one who'd helped two babies into the world.

'Brilliant progress, Summer. Nice and gentle now,' he said, and he saw Ellie's surprise as he came to stand beside her in a supportive role instead of as the accoucheur. 'You're doing fine, Ellie. I'll just watch.' He winced as he saw Anthea's eyebrows nearly disappear into her fringe.

Even Ellie sent a brief look at the other sister's scowling face before she returned her attention to Summer. Slowly, with only an occasional quiet spoken word, the birth was completed. Twin one became Emily and then with another gush of fluid fifteen minutes later, twin two became Aimee.

A rippling sigh echoed round the room as the placenta was expelled. It was one large piece the size of a dinner plate with two umbilical cords, which meant the girls were identical.

Summer sighed into the bed in relief and her daughters lay curled one on each breast as Luke tucked the blankets around them all. 'They're so warm on my skin,' she said, and met her husband's eyes. His were bright with tears and even Anthea looked touched by the moment.

'Good job, Ellie.' Luke's words were softly spoken and Ellie felt the warmth in her cheeks. Typical Luke. Not many doctors would have given up the glory of a twin birth to the midwife. Ellie couldn't help but wonder why he had or if Anthea would have taken the opportunity. 'Thanks for the chance,' Ellie said. There had been a moment there when the closeness they'd had ten years ago had seemed to glow around them.

'Would you like a stethescope?' Anthea attracted Luke's attention and the spell was broken.

Luke listened to both babies' hearts as they lay with their mother, and professed them healthy.

'We'll have a better look once they've had some time with their parents.' He nodded to Anthea and Ellie to draw them out of the room and allow the Browns some privacy.

'You may as well bring the dirty instruments out with you, Ellie.' Anthea's suggestion was all help and smiles and Ellie just did what she was told. By the time she'd wheeled the steel trolley out of the door, Anthea was up the hallway with her arm tucked into Luke's. Ellie's nausea must be early this morning because the sight made her feel slightly sick.

It was only two a.m. Ellie yawned and pushed the trolley into the sluice room. She'd kill for a coffee but wasn't enamoured by the idea of becoming the unwelcome part of a threesome.

Anthea squeezed Luke's arm as they walked up the corridor. 'I think it's time you and I had another serious discussion,' she said, and squeezed again. 'But not at this hour of the morning. I'll make dinner on Monday night. Please, come.'

Luke nodded. He'd been having serious reservations about his engagement, and Anthea deserved to know that. He would have preferred to have waited until he was clearer in his mind about his chances with Ellie, but marriage to Anthea would never work with the ghost of Ellie now a flesh and blood woman. It was not a conversation he relished at this moment, but he owed it to Anthea. 'OK. I'll be there. What time?'

She gave him a level look. 'Tomorrow about seven would suit me if that's all right with you.'

He looked down at her walking beside him. It only seemed like days ago he had believed he was eager to settle his affairs with Anthea. But suddenly life was different and he couldn't believe he was willing to forgo a decent relationship for lust of another woman. Anthea was right. She deserved the truth.

'Tomorrow will be fine.'

Ellie was surprised when she heard the outside door shut after Luke. It had only been a couple of minutes since they'd left her. Bad luck, Anthea, Ellie thought grimly. Then she decided that must be why she hated night duty. She became such a bitchy person without proper sleep.

Five minutes later Anthea actually came to help clean up the birthing suite while Summer was in the shower. Ellie eyed her warily as Anthea stalked around the birthing unit and washed down the bed in quick circular movements. She kept glancing at Ellie and seemed to be waiting for her attention. Ellie stopped restocking the delivery trolley and looked up with forced interest.

Anthea raised one eyebrow. 'Isn't Luke a wonderful person?'

'He certainly seems to care about his clients,' Ellie said carefully.

Anthea smiled but there was no amusement in it. 'I mean as a man. He's handsome, kind, rich...' She paused and made sure she had Ellie's attention. 'And we plan to get married this year.'

'Are you trying to tell me something, Anthea?' Obviously the other woman was picking up on Luke's attention to herself, and Ellie couldn't blame her. If the positions had been reversed, Ellie would scratch Anthea's eyes out. Ellie froze for a moment as she recognised the jealousy that had prompted that thought.

She received another humourless smile from Anthea. 'Stay away from him.'

Ellie shook her head wryly. I wish. Maybe she did need to get out of this town and the vicinity of Luke Farrell, but Cleopatra wasn't going to evict her.

'You're kidding me. I work with the guy three days a week in the surgery and maybe two nights a week here. But if you mean don't seduce him, then I wouldn't dream of it.'

That wasn't strictly true. Because she really couldn't guarantee she wouldn't dream of it. But, Ellie sighed, Anthea's point was taken. They were engaged to be married and Anthea was only protecting her property. Ellie felt incredibly tired.

Anthea nodded once, apparently satisfied she'd stated her intentions. 'Thank you, Ellie.' The phone rang at the nurse's station and a suddenly reasonable Anthea went to answer it.

Ellie stared after her. Anthea was still a strange woman. But if Luke has decided she was the woman for him, then there must be good in her somewhere. And Luke deserved someone who appreciated how wonderful he was. Ellie appreciated him but her loyalties lay with Josh.

The rest of the night flew as Ellie assisted Summer to balance the twins for simultaneous breastfeeding back on the ward.

'You were incredible, Summer,' Ellie said as she rolled the two cots close to their mother's bed afterwards.

'It was my best birth yet and I'd heard a few horror stories about twin pregnancy births.' Summer laughed. 'But they reckon the person who cares for you in labour is such a big influence on how well your labour goes.' She shook her finger at Ellie. 'You were terrific and I think we're a great team. Don't you?'

Ellie laughed. 'The best. Now, try and get some sleep as these two princesses here will be waking you for a feed again soon.' She leaned over and turned off the light. 'If by some miracle they don't wake before I go off, I'll catch up with you at the clinic. We have to get some Grannies organised for you.' She rolled the room door partially closed and walked back down to the birthing unit to finish cleaning up.

The sun rose on Saturday morning not long before Ellie finished work. The air was pleasantly cool but it had the feel of late summer in it and she slid her sunglasses out of her bag to shield the glare from her eyes.

A black BMW reversed into the parking spot next to hers and the next thing she knew Luke was standing beside her.

'Good morning, Ellie.' His voice was cheerful for a man who had been up through the night and Ellie couldn't help smiling back at him. He looked delicious in a high-buttoned shirt and dark trousers. Someone she'd love to curl up with when she crawled into her bed. Then she remembered he was Anthea's.

Her eyes widened and she shot a look at his face again to see if he'd read her thoughts. At that moment she tripped on the edge of the gutter and would have ended up at his feet if he hadn't shot a hand out to steady her.

'Don't go to sleep before you get home,' he quipped, but his hand didn't let go. It could still have been the fault of night duty, but she seemed to be staring at his long fingers around her arm unable to drag her eyes away. Why did she suddenly wonder if she might have missed out on the greatest love affair of all time?

'Hello, earth to Ellie.' His hand dropped and she shivered involuntarily at the loss. But it woke her out of her daze.

'Sorry, Luke.' She took another couple of steps until she reached her car and then turned back to him. 'Maybe I'm a closet epileptic. I think I'm having staring attacks from lack of sleep.' She blinked hard a couple of times.

'I could call you Ellie Petit Mal—it has a nice ring to it.' He smiled at her and she warmed from her toes to the very short hair on her head. 'Go to bed, Ellie. I'll see you on Monday.'

'Night,' Ellie murmured as she opened her car door.

Luke watched her drive away. He didn't really think the jolly approach had worked at establishing rapport between them. He still wanted to draw her into his arms and keep her safe. And she was strange this morning. He hoped she hadn't taken on too much. Josh seemed a great kid but it must be hard being a single parent. From what he'd seen, it didn't look like the boy's father had provided much for them before he'd died, and Luke had to fight the urge to offer help.

Luke turned to stare at the steps to Maternity. He'd promised Anthea he'd do his rounds early before she went home. She'd have a coffee waiting for him and he'd better go in. She probably wouldn't talk to him after tonight but in all honesty he was falling back under Ellie's spell more each day.

Ellie shifted from lying on the lounge to resting her head on her hands at the table as Josh chattered through the day. He didn't seem to mind that his mother was quieter than normal, but by the afternoon Ellie was sick of feeling like a dishrag. She needed some exercise and some energy.

So she mowed her lawn, the Judds' lawn and pruned some of the tangle of overgrowth in the back yard. She still didn't feel any better than she had that morning but Josh had a great time.

Ellie paused to drink a mouthful of water and wipe her brow. She was awake, right enough. But that dull ache she'd discovered in her chest after Anthea's announcements refused to go away. She reached for the clippers again. There was a certain satisfaction in snipping. What she needed was a friend.

Not a male one!

On Monday morning, Belinda Farrell turned up for her appointment half an hour earlier than booked. Ellie welcomed her with open arms into her room.

'Hi, Belinda. It's great to see you. And we've got some time to talk about your labour.'

Belinda smiled shyly at Ellie's effusive greeting and held out her arm to have her blood pressure taken.

Ellie wrapped the cuff around her upper arm and quickly did the observations. Belinda's blood pressure was a little higher again than last week but still not dangerous. 'Are you getting enough rest, Belinda?'

The young woman shrugged. 'What's there to do? I live alone in a small flat and watch television.'

Belinda stood on the scales and she'd gained two kilograms in a week.

Ellie wrote it down and then sat beside her. 'Have you noticed that your feet are more swollen?'

Belinda nodded. 'I had to buy a pair of those slip-on shoes because all the strap ones cut into my feet.'

Ellie frowned and marked that on the card. 'Sometimes pregnant ladies get a condition called pregnancy-induced hypertension, PIH. In the old days it was called eclampsia and it can be very dangerous. Your blood pressure is a little higher again this week and now you have the swelling of the feet. If you get a sudden bad headache above your eyes...' she indicated her forehead '...or blurred vision or even a pain in the chest, sometimes it means your blood pressure has taken a turn for the worse.'

Belinda nodded that she understood. Ellie went on, 'You have to ring us here, or Luke at home or the midwives at the hospital so that we can get you checked out.'

Belinda's eyebrows rose. 'Even in the middle of the night?'

Ellie nodded emphatically. 'Absolutely.'

Belinda shrugged. 'OK.'

Ellie relaxed slightly. 'So, where do you live? Do you have any friends or neighbours that visit you?'

'Not really. I just watch the soaps. I wish Travis had never come back here to live, but with the baby coming I don't have the energy to move back to my old home.' She shrugged tiredly. 'There probably isn't anyone I know there now anyway.'

'Well, you know me, and I'm here. And if you visit

my house you can meet my son, Josh. He's four and will talk you under the table if you get bored at home.'

They smiled at each other and Ellie pulled out a pregnancy diary that she'd found in the newsagent's for Belinda.

'I found this really cute little book which I'd like you to have. It's got pictures of your baby as it grows inside and talks about how labour works with lots of diagrams. It even has a section for a birth plan. Read it and we'll talk about any questions you have next week.'

'Ellic...' Belinda looked up and met Ellie's eyes. 'When I said last week that I wasn't worried about labour...' She paused and drew a deep breath. 'Actually, I'm terrified. Plus, I think Travis's mother thinks she's coming in to be there for the birth. I don't want her to be.'

Ellie bit her lip. Unless the woman had changed a lot in the last ten years, Luke's mother would be the last person Ellie would want with Belinda in the birthing unit. 'Have you told Luke this?'

Luke came to the door and poked his head in. 'Sorry, girls. Was just walking past and heard my name. Told me what?' Belinda paled and Ellie stood up and frowned at Luke, trying to get the message to him that his timing was bad.

'I'm sorry, Luke. I'd really appreciate a chance to discuss something with Belinda in private, if that's possible? Perhaps you could give us a few minutes?'

'Sure,' he said, but the look he shot over Belinda's bowed head promised an inquisition later. He deliberately shut the door to the tiny room as he moved away.

'I'm sorry, Belinda. Go on if you want to.' The silence

in the room lengthened but Ellie didn't want Belinda to feel she had to say more if she wasn't comfortable.

Belinda shook her head and looked down at the floor. 'I was saying I don't want his mother to come in. I just kept hoping she'd forget about it, but she rang me yesterday and said to make sure to ring her and she would drive me in when I went into labour.' Belinda twisted her wedding ring around on her finger. 'I didn't know what to say.' She looked up and Ellie could see her lip was trembling. 'But I don't want her there.'

Ellie put her arm around Belinda's shoulder. 'Don't worry about it. I'm sure Luke can help with this.'

Belinda shook her head. 'Don't tell Luke.'

Ellie winced at the division in loyalties that would involve, but Belinda was oblivious to Ellie's problems.

Belinda bit the skin on the side of her finger. 'Just don't. Or he'll hate me, too. I know they all blamed me when Travis disappeared, but if Travis wanted to disappear it would have been because of his mother hounding him to do better—not from anything I ever did wrong. That woman just got worse when she found out I was pregnant and it was driving Travis mad.'

Ellie squeezed the thin shoulders under hers. 'Nobody blames you for an accident. I think you're fabulous, the way you've kept going after this tragedy. Believe me, I know what it's like to lose someone you love and at least I had a chance to say goodbye.'

Tears seeped from under Belinda's lids and Ellie felt like joining her. 'I'm sorry for upsetting you, Belinda.'

Belinda wiped her eyes on her arm and it underlined just how young she was. 'I'm not crying because of that.

It's because you're so nice to me and I'm just not used to it.'

Ellie sniffed and smiled. 'Good. Then I can stop crying, too.' They both started to laugh, funny, hiccuping laughs with a hint of tears in them. They both stood up and Ellie opened the door. Luke was just going past with his coffee-mug.

'Hello again, you two,' he said. 'What's so funny in there?'

They both stopped so abruptly that they looked at each other and started to laugh again. Ellie grabbed a tissue and blew her nose. 'Girl stuff,' she said, and Luke gave her a searching look.

'Well, if you're finished, perhaps you'd like to come through now, Belinda.'

Ellie quickly wrote on one of her smily cards and gave it to Belinda. 'Here's my phone number and address. Give me a ring if you want someone to talk to or I'll catch you same time, same place, next week. We still need to go through some labour stuff.'

'Thanks, I will, Ellie. Bye.' Luke looked surprised at Belinda's enthusiasm and Ellie just smiled.

At the end of the day's work, Luke came into the nurse's room and leaned on the doorframe. Ellie wished he'd caught up with her outside, maybe in the car park where his presence was diluted by some space and options for escape.

'You seem to be getting along with Belinda well,' he said.

Ellie fiddled with the pens and squared the papers beside the computer. 'It's my job and, besides, I like her.' She avoided his eyes.

Luke took a step closer. 'Is there anything you need to tell me that will affect her coming birth?'

Ellie shrugged and closed down her computer, trying to pretend she wasn't affected by his nearness. Guilt niggled over Belinda's problem with Luke's mother because she'd promised not to discuss it with Luke. 'We have something in common. We both experienced pregnancies after our husbands died.'

Luke stepped back and his voice softened. 'So how long before Josh was born did your husband die?'

'Two weeks. He tried so hard to hang on but there just wasn't time. He'd refused chemo until I fell pregnant and he became very ill so quickly.'

Luke sat on the client's chair and Ellie turned to face him. She leaned her back against the desk with the computer to keep as much space between them as possible because she wouldn't want him to hear her heart racing.

'That must have been hard. So who was with you when you went into labour?'

The sympathy in his voice brought a lump up in her throat. 'My mother stayed with me, but she left as soon as Josh was born.'

Luke shook his head. 'How is your mother?'

Ellie laughed. 'Still the same. She's still bitten by wanderlust and permanently searching for greener pastures.' The opportunity was there for some information. She shot a look at Luke. 'And how's your mother?'

'Older. Perhaps more bitter since Travis died.' Ellie winced at that unattractive picture but didn't say anything. He went on, 'I think she's expecting Belinda's baby to fill a void.'

Ellie had to at least try to help Belinda. 'And do you think that's healthy?'

He sighed. 'I'm hoping that she'll see no one will replace Travis but I do think it's an opportunity for her to soften with a new grandchild.' He stood up. 'Enough about my mother. I know you didn't get on with her but she's really quite aged now.'

He had no idea what the old witch was capable of. Ellie shook her head. 'She hated me, Luke. I'm wondering if she has any softer feelings for Belinda.'

He looked surprised and she had to admire his loyalty. 'She loves Belinda. She told me. Besides, my mother never hated you, Ellie. In fact, she passed on your message about your new and exciting life and career in Sydney to me and seemed very pleased for your happiness.'

Ellie shook her head. Would that be the same day she told me you were married? Ellie thought bitterly, because Ellie had certainly been single with every intention of meeting up with Luke again when she'd made that phone call. Ellie wondered if she would regret her decision to tell Luke. But it wasn't just her younger self and Luke that had been affected by Elsa Farrell. It was Belinda as well. Luke needed to know what his mother was capable of.

Ellie turned off the computer and grabbed her bag for a quick get-away. She took a deep breath and hoped she wasn't doing the wrong thing. The words spilled out into the tiny room like hard pebbles. 'The only time I spoke to your mother on the phone was five years ago when I rang to talk to you, to talk about coming back to Bell's River and you. She told me that you were happily married and expecting a child.'

She watched Luke's eyes narrow as he weighed up what she was saying. 'I married Steve a month later because he needed me.' His expression hardened but he didn't say anything.

Ellie pushed past and opened the door to the car park, knowing he wouldn't be able to follow her because he had to lock up. She just hadn't planned on him walking out after her.

She felt his hand on her shoulder and before she could shrug him off he'd spun her around to face him. The look on his face stunned her. His other hand came up to secure her other shoulder and he gave her a little shake so that she dropped her handbag.

Luke felt as if he'd been hit by a giant fist. He shook his head in denial. 'I don't believe my mother would deliberately sabotage my relationship with you.' He'd told his mother how he'd planned to marry Ellie and she'd never said anything against the idea. She hadn't said much but he couldn't remember her expressing disapproval. 'You must have misheard her.' His voice was harsh.

And Ellie certainly hadn't waited to marry. That didn't sound like a woman that had been coming back to settle in Bell's River. 'Are you saying you planned to come back here and meet me as we'd arranged? That you didn't deliberately change your mind?' He shook his head in denial that his dreams could have been that close. It wasn't possible. His mother wouldn't knowingly have destroyed his happiness.

He laughed harshly. 'How can I believe that? Especially if you married a month later?' His grip tightened.

'Perhaps you should just admit you decided not to come back instead of blaming my mother.' He stared implacably into her eyes. 'I never saw you as dishonest.'

Ellie closed her eyes and he barely heard her whisper, 'How dare you blame me?' She opened her eyes and glared at him. 'I won't have you call me a liar.'

Her teeth were gritted. 'Your mother told me you were married. You can believe me or her. That's your choice. I'm sorry, but maybe it's all for the best anyway. Who knows? It's in the past. I just want you to realise that your mother doesn't always have the best interests of her sons' girlfriends in mind.'

She wriggled out of his grasp and faced him. 'If I'd come back here I wouldn't have Josh, and I could never regret him in my life.' She stepped back a pace. 'But at this moment I regret you in my life.'

Luke flinched and then his arms shot out again. 'Then regret this, too!'

CHAPTER SIX

LUKE pulled Ellie against him and clamped her arms against her sides.

His head lowered and he felt her twist under his hands as she struggled to escape. When his lips captured hers, he wanted to stamp the fact that she should have been his so that she would never forget who hadn't come back to whom. Suddenly the fight went out of her. His anger disintegrated as she sagged against him, and he softened his mouth. The scent of her, the taste of her, the feel of her body against his—it was all he'd wanted since she'd walked into his surgery and back into his life.

To Ellie's disgust, she'd relaxed against him and her anger, and hurt and confusion were lost in a haze of feelings and emotions that welled up from a place she'd thought locked away for ever. When his mouth softened, so did his hands and they swayed together in a cocoon of memories from the past and she never wanted him to let her go. She could feel the sting of tears behind her closed eyelids and her heart felt like it was being squeezed in a vice.

It could have been seconds or minutes later, she didn't know, but then he released her, though not completely or she would have fallen. But her life had changed for ever, because the way he made her feel had stayed the same—and she couldn't deny it.

'Damn you, Luke,' she said. She had to get out of here. 'I'm going to get my son.'

Ellie walked quickly to her car and it seemed to take

for ever to open the door, start the car and reverse out of the car park. Luke watched her the whole time and she tried not to look in his direction. When she glanced in the rear-view mirror as she drove out she could see him still standing in the car park with his hands thrust in his pockets as if he were carved of stone.

Ellie couldn't believe he'd taken his mother's word over hers. It hurt. But not as much as that kiss had pierced her soul.

At seven p.m. that evening Luke knocked on Anthea's door. She didn't smile and he kissed her gently before following her through to the dining room. The room seemed stuffier than usual to him and he wondered if it had always been like this.

They both sat at the table and there was silence for a moment before Anthea broke it. 'I have something to say, Luke.'

He nodded and she went on, 'I'm not happy that you've hired that woman for the surgery. I want to know if you'll consider letting her go. I can see there is still some connection between the two of you and I need to feel secure in our relationship for it to work. Would you do that for me?'

Luke could sympathise with Anthea and it made what he'd come here to say even harder. 'I'm sorry, Anthea. I won't fire her. I can't help my feelings for Ellie but I can't deny my awareness of her. That's why I'm here. I don't believe it's fair to you to continue our engagement when I still have those feelings for...Ellie. I'm sorry.'

He heard Anthea's sudden intake of breath and he shook his head. 'You deserve more than I can give you. I'm not comfortable with the way Ellie makes me feel.'

Anthea had herself back under control. She raised her

sculptured brows and met his look. 'Your honesty is one of the reasons I feel safe to align myself with you. Perhaps you're being hasty? I'm willing to continue our engagement while you sort yourself out. You're a man…' Her shoulders lifted in a tiny shrug. 'She's attractive in an earthy way and once you thought you loved her. Maybe you'll find she isn't everything you thought she was. She's different to us. I am what you see and I'm here for you when you realise that.'

Anthea had missed the point. When Ellie had been gone for ten years Luke had decided that a calm and rational marriage would be good for him. But he could never believe that now. And after kissing Ellie today, he knew she wasn't immune to him. Trying to make Anthea understand was worse than he'd imagined it could be.

He reached across the table and put his hand over Anthea's. 'You're more than I deserve but I will never be the same man I was a month ago.' He smiled wryly. 'Keep the ring. Make it into earrings or a necklace.' He stood up. 'I won't stay to dinner, if you don't mind. I need to think.'

Anthea caught his arm and he stopped. 'I just hope you don't find yourself more unhappy with this woman than you were before. She'll probably leave in a few months and then where will you be?'

Luke looked down at the woman he'd nearly married and knew without a doubt he had done the right thing in breaking their engagement. 'Exactly where I deserve to be.' He leaned over and kissed her cheek. 'Goodbye, Anthea.'

At eight o'clock that night, Ellie's doorbell rang. It was Luke.

She'd had a premonition he would come. Ellie could

see his silhouette through the glass in the door and he looked tall and solid and she could still feel the pressure of his lips on hers. She didn't know whether to open the door or pretend to be in bed, though the latter option was hard to make convincing with the lights still on. But cowardice had never been her style.

He rang the doorbell again and she knew he wasn't going to go away. At least Josh was asleep. Ellie was glad of that as she opened the door.

'Hello, Luke.' His face was unsmiling and she sighed. This wasn't going to be easy. 'Come through into the sitting room.'

The room was furnished with an old club lounge that had come with the house and a couple of small round tables that Ellie had found in a thrift shop. Ellie had draped colourful sarongs over the dull fabric of the lounge and a hand-stitched rag rug lay vibrantly on the floor. Several unframed tropical posters adorned the walls. All easy-to-pack stuff that rolled or folded into her car when she moved on. But the overall look was remarkably bright and homely.

'Most of the furniture came with the house.' She shrugged. 'I move too often to collect many things. Too like my mother, I guess.' She was rambling and she clamped her jaw shut to stop the words.

Luke walked across to stare at a poster of a sandy cove. It looked a lot like the cove at Bell's River. He was still coming to grips with the concept that there had been a possibility she could have come back to him five years ago. And all the might-have-beens that would have involved.

'I spoke to my mother again and she flatly denies she told you I was married. She said you must have misunderstood.'

Ellie shrugged. He didn't believe her so it wasn't important. 'Why aren't I surprised?' She looked at him. 'What do you think, Luke?'

He ran his fingers through his dark hair. 'You must have misunderstood her. But a lot has happened in your life in the last five years.' He looked at two photo frames—one with a photo of Josh and one with a fair-haired man. 'Tell me more about your husband.'

Ellie sighed. 'There's nothing else to tell. Steve was a gentle guy and my best friend. When I told him you were married...' she took in his lack of expression and shrugged '...Steve said it was fate. That we belonged together and that he'd found out he was sick. Acute lymphocytic leukaemia. He was due to start chemotherapy and if he didn't have children then, he never would. They didn't give him much hope and he wanted a child more than anything. So we married and Josh was conceived. It was a tragedy Steve never saw Josh. Josh is very like his father and the light of my life.'

She met Luke's eyes. 'I grew to love Steve and losing him was the hardest thing I've ever had to experience. I'm not setting myself up for that risk again.'

She acknowledged to herself that if she fell in love with Luke she'd never survive losing him.

Unintentionally, the next thought came out loud. 'So it's good that you have Anthea.'

He looked startled, as well he might.

Luke tilted his head as if trying to work out her thought processes. 'Anthea and I have broken our engagement as of tonight.'

Bully for you, Ellie thought. She was too scared of falling in love with Luke to think that was a good thing. 'I thought the two of you were well suited.' What about their boring children? a sarcastic voice in her head whispered. She sat down on the lounge and indicated the chair opposite. She didn't want to get into a discussion about Anthea or why he'd broken up with her. That was too dangerous. 'Sit down and let's talk about Belinda.'

Luke folded himself into the wing chair and crossed his ankles. 'I have no intention of talking about Belinda when my head is spinning with the ramifications of a phone call you may have made five years ago. I came to talk about us.'

'There is no us.' She gave him a level look and the strength he'd glimpsed in her as a teenager had matured into that of a formidable woman. Despite her words, he wanted her even more.

She leaned back in the chair. 'What do you want, Luke?'

'I want to apologise for this afternoon.' His lips twisted wryly. 'I didn't think there was any caveman in me but perhaps you bring out the worst in me.'

Ellie's laugh was bitter. 'Sure. Blame me for that, too.'

He shook his head impatiently. 'I didn't come here to fight with you. I wanted to see you in your home setting. I wanted a chance to talk to you without a patient waiting or a baby crying.' He sat forward in his chair and pinned her with his eyes. 'I also wanted to see if that crazy attraction that I remember from ten years ago is still as strong as it was then. After today I'm not sure that it isn't.'

Her gaze slid away from his and her voice held a tinge of exasperation. 'We're not children now, Luke.'

His smile was gentle. 'I wasn't a child then.'

He watched her soften as the memories returned to both of them. 'I felt like I was older than you,' she said.

'They say women mature younger than men. But I never forgot you, Ellie.' He shook his head as if to further deny he'd forgotten her. 'Why didn't you just come back and see me, like you'd promised? We could have talked, got to know each other again. It didn't occur to me you wouldn't come.'

She gave a harsh laugh. 'I was going to. But we'd been so young when we'd made that silly vow. The older and wiser me decided that it would be safer to phone first rather than turn up and accidentally meet your wife or kids or whoever could have been in your life at that time. When your mother told me you were married I believed her because I half expected it to be true.'

He shook his head again at the picture she painted. 'I became caught up in work after I finished med school so I was busy enough, but there was never any other woman. My brother Travis had begun to show signs of wanting to break away from home. But my mother was fighting his independence until he just ran away as soon as he finished high school, and it affected my mother badly. Everything went haywire for a while.

'When the time had passed for you to come back, I realised I should have more actively pursued you, but I'd promised to let you achieve your goals without ties. By the time I realised you mightn't come back, my mother told me that you'd rung to say you weren't. So instead I just dived back into the work. That's when I decided to make a clean break and complete some more training in England.'

Ellie wished she could have been there for him but maybe it was all for the best. The love she'd had with Steve had been warm and companionable and soothing. It hadn't invaded her personal space. But she had the suspicion that if she ever let her head go with Luke, she'd have no control.

Their differences would clash and mesh and explode,

and if she lost him, like she'd lost Steve, she'd just fade away and die. Then where would Josh be? She couldn't survive something of that magnitude. Maybe she was a coward after all. She knew her strengths and this was one weakness she wasn't going to expose herself to. Josh was the most important person in her life.

'We're both different people to the people we were ten years ago, Luke. Josh and I are happy as we are. I enjoy working with you, let's leave it at that. I don't want a man in my life again.' She could feel the weak tears threatening and stood up to show him out.

He had no choice but to stand as well but she wished he hadn't come up so close to her. 'I don't believe that. Or that you don't feel anything for me now.'

She edged away from him towards the door. 'Despite what I said today, I'll always have a warm place in my heart for the memories of a teenage love, but that window of opportunity has closed and I don't want to go there any more. I could never be your homebody-doctor's wife, serving on hospital committees and growing old in Bell's River as a respectable citizen. And that's what you want, Luke. I was never that.'

'I disagree. You could be yourself and everyone would love you. I'm not giving up Ellie.' His voice wasn't loud but the conviction in it terrified her. He glanced around the room and then back at her waiting to show him out. 'I'm sorry I came unannounced. Despite everything, it is good to see you, Ellie.'

She could feel the tears behind her eyes and she turned away to open the front door. 'It's good to see you, too, Luke.'

He kissed her gently on the lips and they both leaned together before she pulled away. 'Please, go, Luke.'

He took a step towards the door and then reached back and took her hands in his. 'Give us a chance, Ellie.'

She couldn't do it. 'I need to think about this,' she whispered. She held her breath and his lashes came over his eyes and Ellie couldn't tell what he was thinking.

His hands tightened painfully for a moment on hers and then he let her fingers slip slowly through his until he wasn't touching her at all. Ellie felt strangely bereft but she couldn't say yes to him when she was so frightened.

'How much time—this time?' His voice was dangerously quiet and Ellie swallowed the tears in her throat.

She said the first thing that came into her head. 'Give me until after Belinda's baby is born.'

When he said 'Why then?', she realised she couldn't say it was to protect Belinda from his mother. 'Because I like Belinda.' Ellie left it at that.

He nodded and stood up. 'Within twenty-four hours of my niece or nephew's birth.'

This time he did leave and she closed the door after him before he even reached the front gate. She leant her back against it. She'd lied. The magic hadn't changed—just her own willingness to take a risk.

Tuesday was busy again. Mavis Donahue came in. It was her due date but labour hadn't started.

'Haven't you got any hints about getting this labour to start, Ellie?' Mavis sat ponderously in the chair and her cheeks were rosy with the exertion.

Ellie smiled at her. 'Only the usual. Good old-fashioned hanky-panky?'

Mavis sighed.

'I'm sick of it and my husband is exhausted.'

Ellie let out a peal of laughter and Mavis grinned with her as Ellie sat down beside her.

'What about nipple stimulation?' Ellie grazed the front of her own shirt as she made a show of brushing her nipples with her fingertips.

'Like I'm going to spend the whole day playing with myself and feeling like a kinky idiot.' Mavis sighed glumly. 'So how often are you supposed to do whatever you do anyway?'

Ellie bit back her smile. 'OK. I'll explain it a little more. Stimulation of your nipples causes release of the hormone that makes your uterus contract. So if you were to twiddle your nipples every couple of hours, or even more frequently, for a couple of minutes, the extra hormone released can cause your uterus to contract—more frequently if you are niggling around—or to start contracting if you haven't had any yet.

'Pregnant ladies go to the toilet frequently, so I'd suggest a couple of minutes of twiddling every time you sit on the toilet. That has the added advantage of no one seeing you and you don't feel so self-conscious.'

Mavis nodded unenthusiastically. 'What about castor oil? I heard that can send you into labour.'

'Can do sometimes,' Ellie said judiciously, 'but it's not very pleasant. There is a case for stimulation of the same nerve that controls your bowel movements and stimulation of your uterus. But, personally speaking, diarrhoea in labour is the pits.'

Ellie smiled. 'I've heard people say Chinese food can send you into labour. I don't believe it—but it's always nice to not have to cook.'

'I want something that would really work,' Mavis said. 'What about that gel they talk about for inducing labour?'

Ellie shook her head. 'You're not a preferred candidate

with a history of a previous Caesarean. Rarely, the gel can make your uterus over-stimulated and Luke may not want to take that risk with a scarred uterus. You want my advice?' Mavis nodded. 'Go for a walk.'

Ellie squeezed Mavis's leg. 'Relax. Stop thinking and stressing about if and when you go into labour. You can't wish yourself into labour, but you can stop your body making it happen by being tense.'

Mavis sighed. 'But how can you forget about something like this?'

'Luke is not going to let you go longer than a week probably because your last baby was so big. So tell yourself that by this time next week you won't be pregnant any more. Drop your shoulders and sigh. It's going to happen, one way or another. And if you can let it all go, you'll probably go into labour. Trust your body. It knows what it's doing and at the moment it thinks there's too much tension around so it can't be safe to go into labour.'

'OK. I'll try. I'll go for a walk and then have a relaxing bath and maybe just cuddle up to my husband tonight.' She grinned. 'We both need the sleep.'

Ellie heard Luke's door open and she stood up. 'Sounds great. I work Thursday and Friday nights at the hospital so I'll either catch you this week or next week.' She hugged Mavis. 'Trust your body and good luck.'

The phone rang and Ellie picked it up. 'Hello.'

'There's a private call for you.' June's voice didn't hold its usual disapproval so maybe their friendship was improving.

'Thank you. Put it through, please, June.' She waved to Mavis.

'Thanks, Ellie.' Mavis turned away and allowed Luke to guide her into his room. He glared at the phone in her hand but didn't look at Ellie. Things between them had been a tad strained since last night's visit, and now he probably thought she had private calls all the time. She shrugged.

It was Belinda. Technically that wasn't a private call anyway, Ellie assured herself. 'Hi, Belinda. What can I do for you?'

'Sorry to ring you at work, Ellie, but I wondered if I could come around this afternoon and have a talk to you. Something really strange has happened.'

Ellie's brows snapped together. 'Are you all right?'

'It has nothing to do with my pregnancy or my health—just something strange.' Her voice sounded breathless and excited.

Ellie consoled herself that Belinda had said it was nothing to do with her health. 'OK. I'll be home at about six. You can have a meal with Josh and me, whatever I bring home for tea.'

'Great. I'll see you then. Bye.'

'Bye.' Ellie broke the connection but stared at the phone in her hand. She wondered what all that was about.

When Ellie went to have lunch with Josh, she thought he looked a little flat. 'You OK, Mr Diamond?'

Josh nodded and yawned. 'Just had a busy morning.'

'OK, sweetie.' Ellie cuddled him up to her as they ate their sandwiches. 'By the way, my friend Belinda is coming to have tea with us tonight. She's having a baby soon and she has a big tummy.'

His eyes brightened. 'If her tummy moves, do you think she'll let me feel it? Jake Smith's mummy has a baby in her tummy and Jake said he could feel it moving inside like a worm.'

Ellie suppressed her smile. 'Wow. That sounds weird. But we'll ask her—OK?' Josh nodded and Ellie collected their rubbish and put it in the bin. 'Well, I have to go, Josh.' She tapped the colourful watch on his wrist. 'See you in four hours.'

She arrived back at work with a few minutes to spare. June was at the desk and the waiting room was empty. There was no sign of Luke.

'How was your lunch, June?' Before June looked away Ellie thought she detected the sheen of tears in her eyes.

Ellie stopped. 'You know, June, we work together three days a week so we should be friends. And I know nothing about you.' June didn't answer and Ellie perched on the side of the receptionist's desk. She stared at her own shoes as if she hadn't seen June's tears. 'Have you any children, June?'

With that, June pushed back her chair, burst into tears and stumbled off to the lunch-room. The sound of the door as it slammed echoed through the surgery. Ellie blinked and sighed.

Now she'd really upset June but the woman had been looking more unhappy every day since Ellie had started work and Ellie hated being at odds with people. She got up and knocked gently on the lunch-room door. 'June. Let me in.'

The lock unsnicked and Ellie pushed open the door. June was leaning on the sink, staring down into the dirty washing-up water. 'That's what my life is like.' She didn't turn around and she ran her fingers through the water. 'Murky.'

Ellie reached past her and pulled out the plug. 'Well, let it go down the plughole.' She put her hand carefully on June's shoulder, half expecting to be pushed away, but June didn't shrug her off. Ellie turned the tap on and fresh water ran down the plughole after the suds.

'Now, that's what life is like. Let the bad stuff go and

fill it again with fresh stuff. Something's wrong and I think you should let it out.'

June let out the closest thing to a laugh that Ellie had ever heard. 'You know, I really wanted to hate you, because I remember the change in Luke when he said you weren't coming back.' She turned to face Ellie. 'But it's just too hard.' She reached over for a tissue and blew her nose. 'I'm feeling better now. Thanks for your concern, Ellie. We'll talk another day.'

June straightened her shoulders and slid past Ellie in the narrow room to return to her desk. Ellie stared after her. June wasn't so bad after all. And as far as work relations went, it was another step forward towards harmony. If she'd realised what June had wanted to share with her, she might not have been so pleased with her day.

CHAPTER SEVEN

'PIZZAS and salad, and yogurt for dessert? Sound OK, Josh?' Ellie stared down at her son as he pushed the half-sized trolley the supermarket supplied for children. He nodded without his usual enthusiasm and Ellie felt his forehead. He wasn't hot.

She was being paranoid. Nurses were the worst for imagining all sorts of illnesses. 'Let's go home, mate. An early night for you, I think.'

Belinda came not long after they arrived home. Ellie had the salad made and the pizza in the oven. Belinda and Josh circled each other for a while but then they found a mutual love of pregnant tummies.

When Ellie walked out of the kitchen with the cooked pizza she could see them both on the lounge, Josh lying with his cheek on Belinda's stomach. They were smiling at the little movements that made his head rise and fall. Josh yawned.

'Come and have your tea, guys. Then it's off to bed for you, Josh.'

'Aw, Mum.' He spoilt his complaint with another yawn.

'I know, but Belinda will come again, won't you, Belinda?'

Belinda nodded at Josh. 'And in a couple of weeks I'll be able to bring my baby for you to see.'

His eyes brightened. 'Will I be able to play with him?'

Belinda and Ellie laughed. 'It might be a her,' his mother said.

'Well, can I play with it?'

'Sure,' said Belinda. 'But new babies sleep a lot and they're pretty floppy. They grow up quickly, though.'

Nobody said much more as Ellie and Belinda munched their way through their tea and Josh pushed his plate away with only one bite taken. 'I'm not hungry.'

Ellie frowned. This wasn't like Josh. 'How about some yogurt?'

His chair scraped out from the table. 'Can I take it to school instead?'

'Sure, honey.' Ellie stood up. 'Excuse us, Belinda. I'll just help Josh get ready for bed. He's almost asleep on his feet.'

By the time she'd returned to the table, Belinda had cleared away and washed the dishes. Leftovers were covered with cling wrap and the kettle was boiling.

'Hey, you're the pregnant one. I'm supposed to spoil you.' Ellie couldn't believe how quickly she'd restored order to the kitchen.

'I hope you don't mind.' Belinda had set two cups out with coffee and milk.

Ellie gave Belinda's shoulders a quick squeeze. 'Mind? I think you're wonderful. Thank you. Let's have some chocolate with this. I've still got some of my neighbour's brownies in this jar.' She stared thoughtfully at the half-full jar.

'Now that I come to think about it, Josh usually eats them all before I can get one. He really is off his food.' She shelved that worry for after Belinda's visit and carried the coffee and cookie jar into the lounge room.

'So tell me what's happened. You sounded quite unnerved when you rang.'

Belinda pulled the big shoulder-bag she'd brought out from beside the lounge and opened it. There was a brown parcel inside. 'This came in the mail today. It was posted locally.'

She lifted the parcel onto her lap and opened the edges of the parcel where she'd folded it back together earlier. 'It didn't have any note—just these baby clothes.'

Ellie watched as Belinda brought out the most finely crocheted baby layette she'd ever seen. The pattern was lace-like in its intricacy and the tiny bonnet, bootees and jacket were in the palest ivory. A hand-stitched ivory dress was folded below the set and a tiny gold bracelet was clamped around two beautifully embroidered bibs. The circular shawl was as perfect as a spider's web. It was a labour of love and must have taken the creator months to assemble.

'I don't know who could have sent it.' Belinda rubbed the soft shawl against her cheek.

Ellie was stunned. 'Do you think it was Mrs Farrell?'

'She'd have put in a note so that I could thank her, And anything she gave a grandchild of hers would have expensive labels on it.' The trace of bitterness reminded Ellie about the other problem. How to keep Elsa Farrell out of Belinda's birth environment and Luke from finding out Belinda disliked his mother so intensely. She rubbed her forehead.

Ellie stroked the shawl. 'What about relatives? Have you got any relatives that know you're pregnant?'

Belinda shook her head. 'I was adopted and both of my adopted parents are dead.'

'What about your natural mother?'

'I tried to find her but she didn't want to be contacted.' Belinda bit her lip then met Ellie's eyes. 'Someone could have bought it already made. The person who sent it doesn't have to be a woman.'

Ellie blinked. 'What are you getting at?'

'They never found Travis's body.' A chill ran down Ellie's neck. Belinda said the words almost defiantly and Ellie suppressed another shiver. The silence lengthened between them and then Belinda started to talk.

'It's not that hard to see. Travis was a good swimmer and he and Luke have swum in that cove since they were children. Don't you think it would be strange for him to drown there?'

Ellie drifted for a moment when she realised that Travis had probably drowned at the cove that she always thought of as hers and Luke's. She glanced back at Belinda who hadn't noticed Ellie's lapse of concentration.

'They kept telling me it was an accident, as if I'd ever think that Travis would take his own life. He got fed up, but he wanted to do so many things. He'd never deliberately put an end to the possibilities in his life.' Her eyes narrowed. 'Though he did say his mother would drive him to do something drastic one day.'

Ellie was struggling to keep up. 'So what has this got to do with the layette?' Ellie didn't think she really wanted to know, but Belinda was her friend and she would stick by her.

'I think Travis is alive.' Belinda stopped suddenly, as if that was the first time she'd heard the words out loud.

She looked up at Ellie and her eyes filled with tears. 'I've always thought that but I've never told anyone. You won't tell Luke I said this, will you?'

Oh, heck, thought Ellie. 'It's OK. I understand. Unless you want me to, I won't say anything about this to Luke.' Another thing she had to keep from him.

Belinda nodded but Ellie had a premonition there had to be more. 'There's another reason that you think that Travis is alive. Isn't there?'

Belinda nodded again. 'The day he disappeared he told me he'd be there for me when the baby was born. No matter what! He said that out of the blue. And I believed him. I've clung to that. And the fact that they never even found the surfboard or the clothes he was wearing either.'

Ellie's eyes widened even though the 'evidence' was extremely flimsy.

Belinda went on. 'I didn't notice about the clothes for a while but when I did I realised that I never had believed he was dead.' She looked at Ellie. 'I tried to tell Luke but he just kept hugging me and saying that he found it hard to believe, too.'

Ellie spoke slowly. 'So if he's alive—where is he?'

Belinda's voice held conviction. 'He's somewhere making a fresh start for us. Somewhere away from his mother's influence!'

Ellie closed her eyes for a second and tried to be supportive. 'That seems a bit extreme to me.'

'You don't understand.' Belinda shook her head. 'When we first got married, she hounded us. Travis was supposed to be studying to be an accountant but he hated it. One day he found a job in a boatyard which he loved. He was building a yacht in his spare time and we were going to sail the South Pacific until we had a family.'

Ellie tried not to sigh at their idealism.

'When his mother found out where he was working she went and saw his boss and the next thing Travis was out of work. Travis said the place we'd have to move to wasn't good enough, so he came home to sort things out with his mother. It was only going to be for a short time until he found another job. But every time it looked like we could move away, something bad happened.

'Then I found out I was pregnant and it looked like

we were going to be trapped for ever unless he could get away and clear our feet.'

Ellie was far from convinced. 'I'm sorry, Belinda. But I don't think that's a good enough reason for Travis to put his family through an unnecessary memorial service.'

Belinda bit her lip. 'You don't know what that woman is capable of!'

Ellie froze. Yes, she did. Meddling in people's lives didn't bother her at all. But the story was still too far-fetched. The doorbell rang at that moment and they both jumped.

Belinda stared as if the ghost of Mrs Farrell was waiting outside and even Ellie felt a little unnerved by the timing. She got up and peered through the glass. It was June. Despite their earlier conversation, Ellie was still surprised to find the receptionist on her doorstep at eight o'clock at night.

June stood at Ellie's door with her hands clasped together as if to stop herself from shaking, and her usually pale face was ashen.

'June?' Ellie opened the screen door. 'Come in. You look really upset again.' Ellie stood back to invite her in but then June saw that there was someone else in the lounge room.

'You've got a visitor,' she whispered.

Ellie lowered her voice. 'Yes. Belinda Farrell is here, having tea with me.'

June stepped back away from the door. 'I'll come back another time. I should have rung first.'

Ellie sympathised with the woman who obviously had something she wanted to talk about. 'It's up to you. You're welcome to join us, or come back another time.'

June shook her head. 'I'll see you tomorrow. I'm sorry for interrupting.' She hurried away and Ellie stared after her. This was turning out to be a very strange day. She went back inside to her other guest.

Belinda was licking the chocolate from the brownie off her fingers. Ellie reached for one herself—she needed a hit of sugar! Thank goodness for Lil Judd.

Belinda took another brownie. 'Who was that?'

'Luke's receptionist.' Ellie frowned at the chocolate stuck on her fingers. 'I'll catch up with her tomorrow.'

'She's a bit of a sweetie, that lady.' Belinda's speech was garbled with food but the meaning was clear enough.

Ellie blinked and leant her head back against the lounge. 'June?' Were they talking about the same woman? 'Isn't that interesting? I would have thought she was usually sour.'

Belinda shrugged. 'She's always really sweet to me, but maybe that's because I'm related to her boss.'

Belinda stayed another half hour and then left. She looked happier now that she had told someone her suspicions about Travis.

Ellie's head was spinning and she couldn't help worrying what she would say or couldn't say to Luke. If by some bizarre chance Travis was alive, then Ellie even felt sorry for the anguish caused to his mother, let alone Luke. How the heck could she keep this from Luke?

But Ellie feared Belinda was clutching at straws that should have been snipped months ago. She hoped her friend wasn't heading for postpartum depression when Travis didn't turn up at the birth. Or worse, even a severe psychosis.

Ellie sighed and went in to see Josh. He seemed to be sleeping comfortably and his brow still wasn't hot when she felt it. She dropped a kiss on his forehead and went into her own room. She'd hear him if he called out, and tomorrow would be another busy day.

* * *

Ellie spent most of the night tossing and turning. A lot of it was to do with Belinda's startling confidences but most of her insomnia could be laid at the feet of Dr Luke Farrell. Then there was Josh's mystery malaise. Ellie felt like the weight of the world was sitting on her shoulders, squashing her into the ground.

In the morning, Josh was well again. He ate his cereal and seemed keen to take his yogurt for lunch, and Ellie scolded herself for being paranoid about his health.

Still, she mentioned his lethargy of yesterday to his teacher. Apparently it wasn't uncommon for children just starting preschool to be really tired for the first few weeks. Ellie felt better but still asked to be contacted if the school had any worries.

It was close to eight-thirty and she hurried into the surgery with one minute to spare then chastised herself for not remembering she should have come earlier to talk to June. But the receptionist's face wore her usual deadpan expression. 'Hi, June. Sorry about last night.'

'That's perfectly all right, Ellie. I'm sorry for intruding.'

Ellie frowned. 'You weren't intruding, and if you'd still like to come around this evening at the same time, I'll be there.'

June stared at Ellie, as if weighing up whether she still wanted to discuss the matter, but then she sighed. Her face seemed to sag from its stern lines into that of a sad old lady.

'Please, don't wait for me but I'll think about your offer.' Then the outside door opened and June looked away.

The first patient of the day was Louise Hollows. Now

at thirty-three weeks, she came bouncing in with a mile-wide smile and a bunch of flowers for Ellie.

'You are my new best friend,' Louise said as she presented the yellow roses, and Ellie burst out laughing.

'Thank you.' She sniffed the roses. 'These are beautiful and I needed a lift. Come through. Sit down and tell me all about it. But I'd better take your blood pressure first before you put it up with sordid tales.'

Louise tried to look prim and offended but still couldn't keep the wicked smile off her face. Ellie quickly did her observations and then folded her hands in her lap and looked expectantly at Louise. 'Well, go on. What did your husband do when you went home and seduced him?'

'He nearly had a coronary to start with, but I convinced him it was for the health of both of us. We've had a delightful week, though we've calmed down a bit now. But there were a few times there we'll probably remember on our deathbeds.'

Ellie clapped her hands over her ears and then took them away. 'And no unwelcome side effects?'

'I did get a few tightenings, as you said I might, but no cramps or pains. We're both very relaxed now.'

'I'm really pleased for you, Louise. And your husband, of course.' Ellie smiled. 'Actually, I'm a little jealous.' She was joking but Louise pounced on the idea.

'Luke says you're a widow and you have a four-year-old.' When Ellie nodded Louise went on, 'He wasn't gossiping, I practically had to extract each answer with a knife, but I suspect he knew a lot more than he told me so I've decided to ask you.'

Ellie eyed the new Louise with some caution. 'Ask me what?'

'If you'd like to come to dinner one evening with us.' She looked hopefully at Ellie.

It seemed a nice idea and Ellie nodded. 'Thank you. I'd like that as long as you don't think it will be too much work for you.'

Louise laughed. 'I do nothing all day and everything will change when the baby is born. I'm always having dinner parties.'

Ellie wasn't sure she needed to be the single woman at a dinner party. 'So there will be other couples there?'

'Probably a few more people, but it's for fun, not business, so don't stress.'

Ellie supposed it was a way to meet people but being with a bunch of couples wasn't her idea of a relaxing night. Then she shrugged. She really liked Louise. They arranged for the following Wednesday at seven. She'd ask Lil if she would spend a couple of hours in Ellie's house while Josh was sleeping.

In his rooms, Luke was having trouble concentrating. Each time he saw Ellie between patients he found it harder to look away. She was so vibrant and happy and his patients loved her. And that kiss had knocked him for six.

He'd spent the night staring at the stars and realised he'd fallen back under Ellie's spell at her job interview. And it was getting harder to imagine life without her every day.

But it was going to be hard convincing Ellie of that. He needed a strategy, battle plans, a counter-attack to her not wanting to see more of him.

By five twenty-five Ellie was clock-watching because Luke had been strange all day. She just knew he was going to corner her after work if she didn't get away smartly. And she wasn't in the mood to talk to him.

The last patient was in Luke's consulting room and Ellie had already turned off her computer. She heard his door open and Ellie picked up her bag and edged towards the exit.

'Ellie?' She jumped, but it wasn't Luke.

She let out her breath. 'Yes, June?'

'I might leave it until after the weekend.' June avoided Ellie's eyes. 'So don't expect me.'

'Fine. I'll see you next week, then.' Ellie could hear Luke locking the front door. 'I have to go.' She opened the back door and called out goodbye to Luke, then scuttled to her car. 'This is ridiculous,' Ellie mumbled as she reversed out of the car park.

By the time she'd picked up Josh and some fish for tea, Ellie was feeling more relaxed. She didn't know what had come over her. Josh was in his pyjamas, colouring in at the kitchen table, and Ellie was wrapping the fish in foil when the doorbell rang. Ellie sighed. She definitely knew too many people in this town.

The woman standing at the door brought back a lot of unpleasant memories. But Ellie wasn't afraid of her.

'Good evening, Mrs Farrell.' Ellie waited. She wasn't going to make it easier for her, even though Luke's mother did look more aged than the ten years that had passed warranted.

'May I come in?' The voice was the same. Well bred, layered with innuendo and superficially friendly.

'If you wish.' Ellie pushed open the screen door and stood back. 'Please, go through to the lounge. I'll be there in a minute.'

Ellie's gut instinct was to keep Josh away from her visitor and she slipped into the kitchen to warn him.

'Just stay in here until Mummy's visitor has gone. We want to have a private talk.'

'OK, Mum.' Josh didn't even look up. Ellie heaved a sigh of relief and closed the door after her.

Mrs Farrell was staring at the poster of the cove that Luke had noticed the other night.

'Is that Bell's River cove?'

'No,' Ellie said shortly. It had just looked so much like it that Ellie had had to buy the print. Ellie waited for the woman to sit down in the chair opposite hers and then she seated herself. 'What can I do for you, Mrs Farrell?'

The brown eyes hardened and all pretence of civility vanished. 'You could leave my son alone.'

It was like Anthea all over again. She really had stirred up some ill feeling by coming back. Elsa Farrell was such a bitter old woman it was a wonder she didn't have an ulcer. Ellie shook her head. 'Haven't you interfered enough?'

'Obviously not. If you've come back.' Mrs Farrell glared at Ellie. 'You are the wrong kind of woman for my son. He tells me he has broken off his engagement to Anthea. He was happy with Anthea and they were a fine couple—until you came back! You'll never fit into his life.' She curled her lip. 'I can't imagine *you* on a hospital committee. You're a transient and he's a conservative country obstetrician.' She stood up and Ellie could see she was shaking. 'My son is too good for you and I've already lost one son because of an alliance to an ill-bred nobody.'

That was almost too much for Ellie. Contempt for herself she could shrug off from the old biddy, but not contempt for Belinda. The woman was so bitter it was a wonder she woke up every day. Ellie struggled with her temper but control was hard won as she stood and then walked to the door to show the woman out. She could think of a hundred scathing things to say to this woman but that would only bring her down to Elsa Farrell's level. So she chose to say nothing, convinced that her actions spoke more than words in this instance.

Ellie opened the door and both women were careful not to brush against each other as the older woman left.

They both saw Luke at the same time.

'Good evening, ladies.' His face was carefully expressionless. 'What a surprise to see you here, Mother?' The question mark at the end of the sentence was clear.

Mrs Farrell tilted her cheek for Luke to kiss and smiled in Ellie's direction, daring her to contradict. Ellie had to hand it to the witch—she couldn't regain her own control that quickly.

'I was passing and thought I'd drop in. I've been upset by the misunderstanding we had on the phone all those years ago and wanted to apologise to Ellie. I think we've sorted everything out now.'

She glanced at Luke. 'But it's time for me to leave. Will I be seeing you later this evening?'

'Not tonight, Mother. Perhaps tomorrow evening, if you haven't any plans.'

She turned towards the gate. 'Goodnight, then, Luke. Ellie.'

Ellie didn't say anything and Luke covered the few steps up the path to her door. 'Has she been here long?'

Ellie counted to ten then gave him a dark look. 'I don't wish to discuss your mother or her visit. We clearly disagree where she is concerned.' She stepped back towards her door. 'What brings you here tonight, Luke?'

'Not what.' He pulled a battered and old-fashioned child's school case from behind his back and shook it until it rattled. 'Who. I've come to see Josh.'

That startled Ellie and she took a step back. 'What has my son to do with you?' A fleeting grimace crossed his face and she winced at her lack of tact.

He smiled grimly and glanced down at the school case. 'I found this full of my old toy cars and I thought he might like them. They live in the bag so even if you have to move, it's easy to pack them.'

His smile was nonjudgmental and Ellie felt herself unconsciously lean towards him.

When she didn't answer he lifted his brows in question. 'Do you mind?'

Ellie couldn't resist him. And she needed something to take her mind off his horrible mother and her visit. But she felt guilty. Josh was off colour and lust for a man was the last thing she should be thinking of. She sighed miserably, but held open the door.

'Come in. He's through here.'

Ellie went through to the kitchen and Luke followed. Josh was sitting up at the table—fast asleep. She cast a worried look at Luke and hurried over to where his head lay on his hands. 'He keeps doing this and it's scaring me.'

'He's probably just tired.' Luke could see that Ellie was upset. 'If you're concerned, I have a good friend, Rob Donald, who's the paediatrician at the base hospital. He comes up here once a week on a Friday to do a clinic—why don't I get you an appointment next Friday and you can get Josh thoroughly checked out? We can do some blood work on Wednesday so that the results are through for Friday.'

Ellie nodded gratefully. 'That would be wonderful. Thank you. I'll put him to bed.'

'Let me.' Luke scooped Josh carefully into his arms and Ellie felt like something tore in her chest. It should have been Steve carrying Josh but the tragedy was that she couldn't wish for it not to be Luke. She hoped Steve would forgive her if he was looking down.

'Which way?' Luke was standing there with Josh in his arms and she was on another planet.

Flustered, Ellie hurried out into the hallway. 'Sorry. This way.' She scooted ahead to Josh's bedroom and turned down Josh's duvet so that Luke could slip Josh into bed.

Luke stepped back and Ellie bent over her son to arrange him comfortably and drop a kiss on his cheek. They left the bedroom door open as they went back to the kitchen and Ellie looked at the half-prepared meal. Suddenly she felt close to tears. 'He hasn't had any tea.'

Luke came across and put his arm around her shoulders and to Ellie it felt so right. 'Did he have breakfast and lunch?'

Ellie nodded and felt better. She drew a shuddering breath. 'You're right. He won't starve, but usually he has such a good appetite. Maybe it's the move that's disturbed his routine. But we've moved before and he's never been tired like this. I can't help thinking of Steve.'

Luke hugged her once and when she didn't respond he stepped back. 'Steve was different. It's probably just starting preschool but it's natural to worry. He's your baby.'

Ellie half laughed at the truth of the statement and looked down at the fish again. 'Would you like to stay for tea?'

CHAPTER EIGHT

'I CAN be persuaded.' Luke tilted his head sagely. 'And the coincidence is that I have a bottle of chilled Sauvignon Blanc in my car right at this moment.'

Ellie gave him an old-fashioned look. 'That is a coincidence.'

'So, if I go out and get it, will you let me back in?' He looked so young all of a sudden she felt like she'd been whisked back ten years.

She blinked and then he was back to the Luke she saw at work. A different man to the one she remembered but one she could lean on if she chose to. But that would involve Josh sharing her with Luke, and Josh had lost one parent's attention before he'd even had it. Romance wasn't something she should be thinking of, especially when Josh was unwell and needed her.

But Josh was asleep. And Ellie needed Luke tonight— just this once.

She looked up at him and slowly she smiled. 'I suppose I have to, seeing as how you're giving me a referral to your friend and not charging me for it.'

Later, Ellie sat dreamily hip to hip on the lounge with Luke, and his arm rested along her shoulders in the most comforting way. Desultory conversation had come and gone, with some easy silences thrown in.

Ellie couldn't pinpoint the gradations of the end product, this ambience, but it felt remarkably right as they sat there. Quiet music played in the background and Ellie sipped at her wine. 'How did we get to this point already?'

'We're fatally attracted and there's nothing we can do about it.' His words were flippant but the tone wasn't, and Ellie stiffened.

'I do not want to fall in love with you, Luke. I'm serious about that. My life is full already and will be for the next fifteen years.'

He turned to look at her. 'Do you really think we can control when we do or don't fall in love?' He'd been trying to fall in love with Anthea for six months and the best he'd been able to achieve for her had been admiration.

When Ellie had turned up at his surgery it had taken ten minutes to fall back in love with her.

It had taken less than a fortnight for him to break off his sensible engagement to Anthea.

And already he knew he had to find a way to ensure Ellie would never leave again. He hadn't been able to control any of it. He hoped to heaven she couldn't either.

'Can't you give us a chance?' he said.

Ellie looked into his face and saw a man that she admired more than any other man. His kindness, compassion and even his loyalty to his mother were all admirable facets of his character. But that wasn't why he was dangerous to her.

If she committed herself to Luke it would be like a holocaust. The fire would consume her as it had ten years ago. Tall, handsome, assured and absolutely besotted by her. She'd felt like a queen when he'd looked at her—which had been a huge improvement on the usual travelling minstrel persona of her teenage years.

But even then, the longer she'd known him the more she'd come to depend on him being there. Until the thought of a day going by without seeing him had frightened her into going to extreme lengths to arrange meetings.

When Ellie's mother had said they were leaving, a part of her had breathed a sigh of relief that she would have to make the break. The other part had cried for a long time.

She didn't need that intensity again. She didn't want to lose who she was, where she was going or all the independence that she craved. And then, when she was nothing but a part of him, she'd be at the mercy of a fickle fate that might whisk him away and leave her behind. It would be a hundred times worse than when she'd lost Steve. She was like a lemming, to have come back here.

She and Josh were a team. And after Belinda's baby was born, they'd leave. She just had to resist Luke for another month. And she would. But she needed him now. She'd finish it after tonight. As if in a dream, she drifted over to close the lounge-room door into the hallway and then turned back to face him.

'Kiss me, Luke.'

He pulled her gently towards him and onto his lap and his arms came around her. She tilted her head to look into his face and was lost. When his lips came down on hers firmly and surely to stake a claim, she drew him into her as if this was her last chance to be a part of him.

He groaned and his arms tightened around her as the kiss deepened and they were swept away. His hand slid from her shoulder to the buttons of her shirt and pushed the material aside to gain access to the softness of her.

When he covered her breast with his fingers she moaned softly for the aching sweetness of it took her breath away. She needed to feel him against her, all of him, skin to skin, and she fumbled with the buttons of his shirt blindly and desperately.

He drew back a little to give her access. 'I want you, too, sweetheart,' he murmured against her lips. 'Let me help you.' He pulled his own shirt over his head and lifted hers off just as easily. She shuddered as he pulled her back against his chest and she rubbed against him like a cat, purring with the delicious sensation of his skin against hers.

When she reached for his zipper his hand stilled her. 'Not here,' he whispered, and Ellie froze for a moment as she tried to orientate herself. Of course. Suddenly her skin felt as cold as ice.

She slid away from his arms and stood up, crossing her hands over her breasts. Feverishly she picked up her discarded shirt and she could feel his eyes on her as she tried to restore her clothing. Ellie realised the depth of his possession of her. She had been so immersed in her feelings for Luke, and her lust for him, that she had been prepared to ravish him on her lounge-room floor.

Regardless of the chance that Josh could come in and see them.

It had started already. Her priorities seemed to be changing, despite her resolve, and Josh's standing was threatened by how she felt about Luke.

And while her son was sick, for heaven's sake. She sickened herself.

She shivered in horror at the thought of Josh finding his mother making love with a man. It was symbolic. She had shut the door against her son. She flung open the door, ignoring Luke's voice as he tried to settle her.

She had to see her son but when she went into his room, Josh was curled up in a ball, snoring softly into his pillow.

'He's been asleep the whole time.' Luke's voice came from behind her shoulder and she shivered as his breath crossed her neck.

She turned to face him. 'I'd like you to go home now, Luke.'

She couldn't read his expression in the dim light of the hallway. He sighed. 'Stop beating yourself up. You're a wonderful mother. But you're also a woman. I'm asking that you give us a chance.'

She met his eyes and enunciated clearly. 'No, Luke. I don't want to give us a chance.'

'Then why did you come back?' His shirt was in his hand and he had his shoes on.

He touched her shoulder until she turned fully to face him. 'And why do we drive each other wild? Because that's what it is. What we have is the real thing.' She didn't answer and he just stared at her. 'I'll see myself out.'

Ellie watched him go and the pain of loss was a timely reminder of just how bad it could get if she let it. The door shut behind him and she sighed and said in a small voice, 'I was a fool to come back.'

When she woke next morning, Josh was beside her. She remembered picking him out of his bed and bringing him into her double bed. Ostensibly, it had been because she'd had some wine and might not hear him if he called out. More likely it was because she wanted the comfort of his small body next to hers.

It was still early and Ellie dozed off again. When she woke at eight, Josh was sitting on the floor, playing with the case of cars that Luke had brought.

'Hello, my love. Have you been awake long?'

Josh shook his head. 'Where did the cars come from?'

Ellie's throat closed over for a moment and she had to force herself to swallow to be able to talk. 'Dr Farrell brought them for you. They were his when he was a little boy and he thought you might like them.'

'That was very nice of him.' The careful wording of the sentence caused a lump in Ellie's throat. She loved Josh so much.

'You could draw a picture of you playing with them as a thank-you. I'll give it to him next week.'

Josh nodded and drove an old station wagon up the side of the bed and onto the covers. Ellie watched Josh park the car next to her hand and then climb down to get another one. When he'd finished, she'd get up and get breakfast.

Ellie stared at the ceiling. She had to get through Thursday and Friday nights and hope that none of Luke's clients went into labour. She had no idea how she would get through the clinic hours when she would be forced to see Luke. She would stay until Belinda's baby was born and then she and Josh were out of here.

That night, Ellie was pleased to see her new friend Sam on evening shift again.

'Hello, Sam. Usual Thursday night for you? How's the ward?' she said as Sam opened the door into the ward.

'Busy. We've an established labour and a prem in the nursery plus the twins.'

Ellie could hear the beeping of the foetal heart monitor from the birthing unit and another higher-pitched beep from the nursery. 'Who's on with me tonight?'

'Anthea.' Ellie grimaced and they smiled at each other.

Ellie crossed her fingers. 'The lady in labour—is it Mavis Donahue?'

'You've got it in one. I keep forgetting you meet these ladies in Luke's rooms.'

Ellie was thrilled for Mavis that she'd come into labour by herself. But that meant Ellie had to see Luke if Mavis's baby arrived during the night. She couldn't decide what was worse—missing out on being with Mavis in labour or having to deal with Luke again.

The night bell rang and someone let Anthea in. Sam waited until the other sister sat down and then dived into report as she was on the quick shift and would have to return in the morning.

'Four patients in this evening. Summer Brown is in room five with the twins. She's doing really well and is looking at going home either tomorrow or Saturday. Both girls are feeding well and gaining weight, although twin one is a little slower than her sister.'

'In room two, Jackie Deverill is yesterday's normal delivery at five weeks early. She's comfortable and getting used to the shock that babies can come at the most inconvenient time. Her boy, at 2400 grams, is doing well enough and we're monitoring him at night because he has a tendency to run some bradycardias. The good news is that he's self-stimulating when his heart rate drops below ninety. He's a tinge jaundiced so we'll have to watch his feeding. If he gets too sleepy he's for an SBR and tube feeds.'

'Baby Carter, now officially Harley, is also going home tomorrow with Mum. Both are doing well. He's almost regained his birth weight and is demand feeding now.'

'In birthing, we have Mavis Donahue. Mavis is term plus two days, has had one previous Caesarean section for failure to progress and has decided she would like to try one more time for a natural birth.'

Anthea made a disgusted noise. Sam stopped and looked in her direction. 'Did you say something, Anthea?'

'Ellie can look after her. She'll be a Caesar. Why on earth would she expect it to work this time?'

Ellie weighed up the energy required to convince Anthea otherwise then decided that Mavis would do it for her. She held her peace.

'As I was saying,' Sam went on, 'Mavis came in at eight o'clock this evening with ruptured membranes.' She turned to Ellie. 'Mavis dilated to five centimetres last time and stayed there until the baby became distressed and needed to be delivered by Caesarean section. Tonight, she coped well until I had to put the CTG monitor on her and she had to lie down.' Again Ellie held her peace. The ward protocol was for a labouring woman to have a foetal heart monitor trace at least twice a shift. Hopefully it would be finished by the time Ellie went in and they could get Mavis up again.

'I've offered her some pethidine but she said she wanted to wait for you, Ellie.' Sam grinned and Anthea turned a basilisk-like stare towards her.

Lucky Anthea had already allocated patients or Ellie had the feeling it would have gone differently.

'So that's the happy family, and if you'd like to come down with me, Ellie, I'll say goodbye to Mavis and hand her over to you.'

Anthea walked stiffly into the nursery and Ellie sighed. Another fun night with Cleopatra.

When Ellie entered the birthing unit Mavis groaned with the strength of her contraction and her husband looked like he was trapped in a nightmare. The foetal heart trace was at least half an hour long and showed the baby was coping well with the labour. It also showed a line of regular contraction hills that were shooting over the graph lines. Sam wished them both luck and left.

Ellie waited for the current pain to subside before she spoke. 'Hi, Mavis. Hard at it, I see.'

'Lord, yes.' Mavis wiped her face with a damp washcloth and sighed into the bed.

'Let's get this off you first,' Ellie said, and her hands busily undid straps and wiped the conducting gel off Mavis's stomach as fast as she could. 'The trace looks great, baby is having a ball and that labour you were hanging out for looks like it arrived with a vengeance.'

'You're telling me. I can't believe I wanted this to happen. Once it started I clearly remembered how rotten it was going to get.'

'Funny, that,' Ellie said. 'Can I just have a quick feel of your tummy and then we'll get you up and into the shower again? See if we can get rid of that tension and extra pain you always end up with when you have to lie on the bed.'

Ellie gently palpated Mavis's stomach and explained the position the baby was lying in. 'Head first, on his side and curled up ready to come out. Everything looks great for baby. Let's get Mum organised.'

Another pain hit before Mavis could sit up and she fixed her eyes on Ellie as she breathed through it. When she started to moan, her husband whitened and Ellie could see there could be more of a problem with him coping with Mavis's pains than with Mavis herself.

'Can't she have an epidural?' He wiped his face and his voice rose. 'Luke said she didn't have to go through this again.'

Ellie smiled gently at him. 'If you can just hang on until this pain is finished, we'll have a talk about it.'

John's eyes were darting all over the room as if the

answer to Mavis's distress was hiding somewhere in the room. 'I don't want to talk about it. I want my wife pain-free. Now!' His face was flushed and Ellie hoped he didn't suffer from blood pressure because he looked like he was going to have a stroke. She needed to get through to him before he panicked Mavis.

'For you or for her?' Ellie's voice was quiet but it dampened his hysteria like a cold washcloth. 'Give her a chance to get into her stride. When she asks for it she can have it. But don't force it on her because you can't stand the noise.'

The shock on his face would have been laughable if there had been anything to be amused about. Mavis completed his day by saying, 'Shut up, John. I can moan if I want to.'

To Ellie's surprise he did laugh then and most of the tension in the room dissolved. 'I'm sorry, love.' He kissed his wife's cheek. 'I lost it for a minute there.'

Mavis didn't have time to waste. 'Get me off this bed, Ellie.' They all heaved until she was upright and leaning on the bedside table. 'Phew,' she said.

'OK.' Ellie was feeling better, too. 'Things are improving. How about the shower, Mavis? Can you handle that until you relax a bit more and then we'll discuss how the pain is hitting you?'

'Let's go before the next one, then.' They nearly made it but Mavis had to stop at the door to lean on John. When she started to moan, Ellie could feel John's eyes on her. 'Think of it as twice the noise, half the pain, and you get to like the moaning.' He gave her a weak smile and when the contraction was over they continued the shuffle into the bathroom.

Mavis looked up. 'I don't know that I'd go so far as half the pain but it does help.' They all smiled at each other and Mavis sat on the big blue ball in the shower recess. The hand shower could be aimed onto her lower stomach and Ellie watched Mavis's shoulders droop as soon as the hot water hit her. 'Ah-h. That is good.'

Ellie thought John was going to pass out with relief.

After a few minutes, when Mavis had regathered her reserves, it was time for tactics.

'So how am I going, Ellie? And don't give me any bull.'

Ellie wanted to hug Mavis for her down-to-earth approach. She wouldn't lie to her either. 'You're doing brilliantly. They said you were four centimetres dilated at eight o'clock so I would expect you'd be at least five or six now.'

Mavis snorted without humour. 'That's what they said last time and it never budged off the five. How can we tell if it's working or whether I'm just going through this agony for nothing and will still end up with a Caesarean?'

Ellie crouched down beside Mavis and ignored the splashes of water on her legs. That was the good thing about not wearing stockings—they didn't get wet. 'Mavis, we talked about this. Five centimetres is your watershed—you have to believe in your body and "see" it opening all the way to allow your baby to come down. Don't let your mind trick you into defeat.' Ellie included John in her pep talk. 'Your contractions are strong, you're as relaxed as anyone could wish for and your baby is pointing in the right direction. Go with the flow and visualise your cervix opening. As the pain gets stronger, see the baby's head pushing you open. And moan. Moaning is a great opening noise.'

'Oh, hell.' John slid down the bathroom wall and put his head in his hands.

Ellie tapped him on the shoulder. 'And you believe it,

too, buster, because there's no room for negatives in this bathroom.'

Mavis started to giggle and John gave a rueful grin. Ellie pushed the shower chair over behind Mavis and gave John a tube of back cream. 'Sit. Rub when she moans and use the same rhythm that she has. Your hands will give her strength and I want you positive-vibing this baby out, too.'

It took a couple of contractions to coach John away from a car-wash type of rub to the rhythmic knead that Mavis liked. And then there was no stopping him. He started to chant, when his wife moaned, 'Opening, opening,' until the pain was gone. Then his hands stopped and all was quiet until the next contraction.

Ellie couldn't believe the turnaround. The phone rang in the birthing unit and she edged backwards out the door without them even noticing she was gone.

It was Luke. 'Hello, Sister Diamond. I understand you're looking after Mavis Donahue. How is she going?' Ellie started to giggle with the relief of it all and Luke's response was unamused. 'What on earth could be funny? John was a mess when he rang me to say they were coming in.'

'He's rubbing her back in the bathroom and chanting at the moment.' Ellie's voice was still unsteady. 'And Mavis is doing well.'

'Has she had anything for pain and how is her CTG?'

Ellie drew a breath and dug for her professionalism. 'No pain relief required as yet and I've only just taken her off the foetal monitor.' Ellie looked at her watch and realised it was almost an hour since Mavis had gone into the shower. She needed Mavis off the bed if she was going to dilate. 'I'd really like to keep her in the shower for a while yet. Is it all right if we keep doing half-hourly intermittent monitoring instead of the cardiotocograph for the time being?' Ellie crossed her fingers.

'If she needs pain relief I want her back on the monitor. I'll ring again in a couple of hours, unless you ring me first.' Then he hung up.

Ellie sighed with relief. The next hour went slowly but they were all in a rhythm. Towards one a.m. Mavis was getting louder but she was dozing between the contractions as her natural endorphins kicked in to dull her senses.

Ellie whispered to John what was happening and he just nodded and rubbed when required. At one-thirty things changed.

Mavis moaned once, very loudly. John jumped and then Mavis stood up and kicked the ball away. She leaned into the shower rail and yelled at the top of her lungs. Ellie's eyes brightened and she stood up from the stool she'd been sitting on.

'OK, Mavis. Sounds like transition. We talked about this panicky feeling and that it only lasts a short time.'

'I want to go home.' She spoke through clenched teeth and Ellie's smile grew. Excellent. John was looking from one to the other and then the next pain hit.

'I can't do this any more,' Mavis wailed, and then her breathing changed. Ellie moved the ball and replaced it with the birthing stool—a fibreglass toilet-like seat with handles on the side and an open front.

'I want to sit down and push.' And Mavis did. She settled on the new seat and hung on for dear life. Ellie quickly checked that Mavis was fully dilated and then sat back.

'She's OK now, John. She's ready to push.' Ellie refilled the cup with ice and put it in front of Mavis. She wet two washcloths with the icy water and offered one to her and the other to John. The cold water made Mavis gasp but then she opened her eyes. 'That was pretty wild. Thanks for the washcloth. All this hot water was giving me a head spin.'

Ellie smiled as John wiped his brow. 'You can't faint now, John, we're getting to the exciting bit.'

He groaned. 'I don't know how much more of this I can stand.'

Ellie looked at him with sympathy. 'I'm afraid you'll have to take as much as it needs. So hang in there and you can all sleep later.'

Within half an hour a small bulge of baby's head was visible between Mavis's legs and Ellie slipped out to ring Luke.

When he answered she was brief. 'Ellie here. Head on view.' And hung up.

She returned to the bathroom and crouched down beside the birth stool. 'Mavis? Do you want to move to the bed now or after your baby is born?'

It took a few seconds for the words to sink in and then Mavis started to get up. 'Let's go now because I doubt I'll want to move when this is over.'

Ellie grinned and helped John move his wife out of the bathroom and across to the bed. She manoeuvred the electric controls until the bed sat upright like a chair. Then she removed the foot of the bed so that Mavis could sit as if she were on a seat. Her feet rested in two footrests near the ground. 'How's that?'

Mavis nodded but didn't speak. She was too busy. Ellie opened the drape on the delivery trolley and hoped Luke would come before she had to ring for Anthea instead. As if conjured up by her thoughts, the door opened and Luke came in. Ellie was glad to see him.

CHAPTER NINE

'WHAT a wonderful sight,' Luke said as he saw that a vaginal delivery was now a certainty for his patient.

'Yeah, right. I must look a treat! Now get it out of me,' Mavis muttered.

Ellie bit her lip to hide her smile and Luke's eyes met hers in brief appreciation of the moment. This wasn't the place for personal problems.

John was pole-axed. He couldn't believe he was going to see his child born. Ellie kicked a chair over to him before he fell down, and he subsided without tearing his glazed expression away from his baby's head.

Ellie's gloves were on but she stepped back out of the way for Luke to take over the delivery.

'Slowly now, Mavis,' he said. 'I know Ellie would have said how good your pushing has been, but can you just puff the baby out gently for this last bit?'

Baby's head seemed bigger by the second and Ellie was quietly pleased that Luke was the one to help the baby out as it looked to be larger than they'd expected. Finally the last of the baby's head was born and Luke slipped his fingers in beside the baby's neck to feel for the cord. He didn't find any and stood back to wait for the next contraction.

'What are you waiting for?' John was staring at the blueness of his baby's face and it seemed to be turning darker as he watched.

Luke's voice was calm. 'The baby will probably be born with the next contraction. It always seems to take a long time when you're waiting for it.' His eyes were kind. 'Most babies are pretty blue when they're first born, especially if they sit like this for a couple of minutes. So don't be surprised if your baby looks pretty ghastly. He or she will cry soon enough.'

Thankfully Mavis moaned with the onset of the next contraction and Luke gently held the baby's head between his hands and tipped it down to allow the top shoulder to slip out of the vagina. Then he lifted the baby's head gently upwards to release the second shoulder. It was quite a tight fit. With a rush the rest of the baby followed in a gush of fluid and within seconds it was lying on its mother's breast before John could comprehend it was all over. 'I've got a baby boy!'

'We've got our boy!' Mavis whispered. She tentatively slid her hands up to hold her baby and Ellie tucked a warmed bunny rug around them both.

Luke attached a plastic clamp around the pulsating cord about two centimetres from the newborn's tummy and then applied the artery forceps another inch down the cord.

'Come on, John. Anyone who can moan like Ellie says you can should be able to cut the cord.'

Dazed, John stood up and took the scissors from Luke. Luke pointed out the spot to cut and John gritted his teeth and did the deed. It was harder than he'd expected and he had to chomp at it with the scissors a few times to sever the link.

'I do not believe that.' Mavis's voice took everyone by surprise. She was staring at her husband who sheepishly handed the scissors back to Luke. 'You cut the cord!'

He moved to the head of the bed and laid his head

down beside the now normal coloured face of his son for a moment. Then he kissed his wife.

'You are the most incredible woman in the world and I will love you for ever. Thank you for my son.'

Ellie bit her lip and turned away. A tear splashed on her hand and she dipped her head to hide the emotion that had soared up her throat at John's words. It was moments like these that made her appreciate she had the best job in the world.

'Well done, everyone,' Luke said. The placenta wasn't ready to come and Luke left it for the moment. He pulled off his gloves and came to stand behind Ellie, and then she felt his hand on her shoulder. It was firm and comforting and warmed her heart. She blinked the remnants of her tears away and nodded, but she still couldn't look at him or she might have broken into the happy sobs that at least would have released the last of her tension from the birth.

Luke lifted his hand and she missed his contact as he moved away towards the couple on the bed. 'Let me listen to baby's chest and then I'll leave you to enjoy your son.' His slid the stethoscope under the bunny rug without moving the baby. Several seconds later he took the stethoscope away. 'He sounds fine. I'll check him properly later when he's in the nursery.'

Anthea poked her head around the door and made eye contact with Luke. She didn't say anything but Luke nodded and soon after that he left the room. It took another fifteen minutes for the placenta to come away and Ellie made the Donahues look at it to appreciate how clever the organ was.

'It's a miniature heart-lung machine. The best man-made one can't even do what this does.' She pointed out the membrane sac that the baby had floated in and raved about the cord.

'OK, Ellie,' John said. 'Enough about that thing.'

Ellie stopped and smiled ruefully. 'Sorry. I love placentas.'

She tidied mother and baby and then left them to some private family time. Ellie believed the first hour with a baby's parents was vitally important and shouldn't be disturbed unless medically necessary, and she needed a few minutes to regroup as well. She slipped into the sluice room to remove her gown and gloves, washed her hands and then wandered up to the tearoom to put the kettle on.

To her surprise, Luke was still on the ward.

'Tea sounds good.' He came into the room and leaned against the bench as she waited for the kettle to boil. 'Well, that was a great outcome.'

'That was exhausting,' Ellie said. 'I just hope no one else comes in because I can't face having another baby tonight.' She grinned as she replayed the words in her mind. 'And I didn't even have to push it out.'

Luke smiled back at her. 'Mavis will be thrilled and I can't believe how good John was.' He shook his head in disbelief. 'He even cut the cord.' Their eyes met and they both started to laugh. It was light relief after all the angst she seemed to be accumulating about Luke, and she savoured it.

Ellie couldn't stop giggling. 'I loved Mavis's response to your comment as you came in the door.'

Luke looked sheepish. 'I can't quite remember what I said but I really wasn't talking about an attractive vagina.'

Ellie bit her lip and tried to control herself. 'I think I

love Mavis.' When she looked up Luke's face was serious and the whole mood in the room changed.

He took a step towards her and her breath stuck in her throat. 'Don't, Luke,' she whispered, but he just kept coming.

'Stop running, Ellie,' he said quietly. This kiss was gentle but searching and a celebration of the birth they'd shared. And it brought the tears to Ellie's eyes again. She could feel her heart splintering inside her and the fear of being lost in him was very real. She stepped back and pushed the back of her hand against her lips.

Luke didn't say anything and with one last look at her turned around and left. She heard the outside door open a few seconds later. Then it closed.

'Where's Luke?' Anthea appeared at the kitchen doorway and searched the room with a glance as if Ellie was hiding him somewhere.

'I think he's gone,' Ellie said, and she turned back to the kettle, which had finally switched itself off.

'He said he was having a cup of tea.' Anthea's voice bordered on accusation and suddenly Ellie couldn't stand it any more. She said the first thing that came into her mind that would get rid of Anthea.

'Maybe he's in birthing again. I'll make my tea and have a look.'

'I'll go.'

Ellie tried to look surprised that Anthea offered. It was a poor effort at subterfuge but Anthea didn't notice as she hurried away.

Ellie considered hiding in the toilet until she had her sense of humour back but that was too much of a cop-out. She took her tea and slowly followed Anthea down the hall. It was going to be a long night and she hoped nobody came in—this time because she couldn't face Luke again.

When Ellie went to pick up Josh from the neighbours early Friday morning, Lil pulled her aside. 'I think this boy is coming down with something.'

Ellie felt her stomach drop. Lil, too! 'Dr Farrell is going to refer Josh to the paediatrician for a check-up next Friday and he's ordering some blood tests on Wednesday.'

'That's good.' The older woman saw the concern in Ellie's face. 'Now, don't you think he was any bother because he wasn't. He's just not his usual self.'

'Thank you, Lil. I'm so lucky to have you and Clem.'

Lil blushed, pleased with the compliment but awkward at the praise. She nudged Ellie away. 'Off you go. I'll see both of you tonight.'

By eight o'clock that night Ellie had settled Josh over at the Judds' house. She'd planned to catch an hour or two's sleep before work. The doorbell rang and Ellie glared in the general direction of the door.

She'd really been counting on that extra rest. She sighed and padded across to look through the glass. Judging by the shape on the other side, June had decided she couldn't wait any longer to talk.

Ellie opened the door. 'Hello, June. Come in.' She could see the receptionist was nervous and she stepped back so that June could enter. She smiled at the older woman. 'I've no visitors and even my son is next door for the night. I have to leave for work just after ten but until then I'm free.'

June darted a distressed look at Ellie's face. 'Were you going to have a sleep before work?'.

Ellie smiled. 'I slept this morning. Now, come into the kitchen and I can make us tea or coffee while we talk. Would you like something now?'

'Nothing, thanks.' June perched on the chair at the end of the kitchen table. 'I'm sorry for intruding, Ellie, but I have to tell someone or I will go stark staring mad. And you were kind to me and I see how the women like you.' June's face was strained. 'My nerves are getting so bad, I'm jumping at shadows. I just need someone who can listen.'

'I'm listening, June, and there's no hurry. Take your time.'

Ellie fixed herself a coffee because she didn't want to yawn in the middle of June's revelations. It also gave the older woman time to settle before starting her story.

Ellie sat down at the other end of the table. 'When you're ready, June.'

'You won't tell anyone what I'm going to tell you, will you?'

Ellie sighed and thought how many things she seemed to be accumulating that she couldn't tell anyone about. She shook her head. 'I promise.'

June stared at her for a moment and then started. 'I suppose I should start twenty-three years ago.' She drew a deep breath. 'I used to work for old Dr Farrell, Luke's father, so I've known Luke and his brother since they were children. He was kind man, just like Luke, and he often invited me to the dinner parties Mrs Farrell used to have.' She looked up. 'I think the doctor invited me because he didn't like a lot of the people Mrs Farrell used to invite.'

She looked down at the table. 'Anyway, I was young and impressionable and fell in love with one of the frequent guests—but he was married.' She looked at Ellie.

'I never planned to be the other woman. But somehow I did become just that for a little while.' She didn't see Ellie's sympathy and went on. 'He told me he was unhappy in his marriage and that he would leave his wife.' She shrugged off a disillusion that had hurt for many years. 'I should have known better.'

She gave a harsh laugh. 'To be even more stupid, I fell pregnant and, of course, this man denied the child was his.' She looked up. 'Twenty-three years ago, it was harder to be a single mother and I didn't know what to do. Mrs Farrell found out and told me to keep my pregnancy a secret. She arranged for my baby to be adopted.'

June wiped the corner of one eye with her finger before going on. 'I didn't want to do that but she said because the man was married the baby would be better off with proper parents.' She looked at Ellie as if for reassurance. 'I wanted what was best for my baby even though it broke my heart. You do understand?'

Ellie shifted her chair so that she was beside June and she laid her hand over June's. 'It must have been terrible for you and I think you were very brave to think of your baby before yourself.'

June blew her nose on a crumpled hanky then went on. 'Anyway, Mrs Farrell arranged for my baby to be born in another town. My baby was a girl and I came back here to live.

'At first I thought Mrs Farrell really wanted to help me, but later on I found out why she didn't want me to have my daughter. She'd been involved with my baby's father, too, you see. He was an irresistible charmer who had a way of making you feel the most important person in the world.'

She shrugged. 'But that doesn't excuse me for falling for him either.' She brushed that aside and didn't notice the wide-eyed look of incredulity that Ellie was giving her.

'Anyway, Dr Farrell gave me my job back when I finally returned. I don't think he knew about my baby, but I was never invited to any more parties—not that I wanted to go!' She shuddered. 'I just wanted to die. But unfortunately I just kept waking up ever morning.'

For Ellie, the sadness that surrounded June had become clear, and she felt guilty for not trying to be more understanding of June's moods in the past.

'Anyway,' June said, 'Mrs Farrell always had that knowledge and she used to ask me things about people, and her husband and her sons, and I had this feeling that if I didn't tell her everything she wanted to know, then she would tell people my secret. Or somehow make something bad happen to my baby.' She looked at Ellie. 'I had to tell her. She's not a nice person, you know.'

'I know.' Ellie nodded. June had stopped for a moment and was gazing down at the table. Ellie ventured a gentle question. 'Did you ever try and contact the adoption agency and find your baby?'

June shook her head. 'Mrs Farrell arranged the adoption and I never knew who took my daughter, so I couldn't. Then one day last year my daughter must have tried to find me and I got a letter from the authorities. I finally knew her name.' She stopped and her voice dropped. 'I couldn't believe it. It was like a circle. She wrote that she was married and she'd married Mrs Farrell's son, Travis!'

Ellie sighed. 'Belinda.' June nodded. 'So *you* sent the layette?'

Tears formed at the corners of June's eyes as she nodded.

'It was beautiful,' Ellie said. 'And she loved it.'

June gave a watery smile. 'Thank you for telling me that.' She blew her nose. 'I started crocheting as soon as I found out Belinda was pregnant.' She bowed her head for a moment and then she looked back at Ellie.

'At first, I tried to think of the best way to tell Belinda, but then I started to get frightened again. Elsa Farrell wouldn't be pleased when she realised my daughter had married her son, and I didn't want her to take it out on Belinda. I'm not much of a mother for anyone. But I can help Belinda without her knowing.'

Ellie frowned. 'It doesn't have to be that way, June. You'll be a wonderful mother and grandmother. I think you should tell Belinda.'

June shuddered. 'But what if I'm not what she expected? What if she's disappointed in me?'

'Did you know that both her adopted parents are dead?'

June nodded. 'I know a lot about her. I get so worried when she doesn't turn up for her antenatal appointments. I keep ringing her and suggesting another day until she comes in.'

One of the other secrets she wasn't supposed to share surfaced, and Ellie sighed. Belinda's state of mind was a real concern to her. June was Belinda's mother—who better to ask help from?

Ellie took a deep breath. 'I'm going to tell you something that Belinda told me, and while I feel awkward at breaking a confidence, you are her mother and might have some way you can help her through this.' She paused and hoped she was doing the right thing.

'Belinda doesn't believe her husband is dead!' June didn't say anything and Ellie frowned. 'She expects him to turn up for the birth of her baby!'

Ellie waited for June's expression of disbelief but it didn't come. Ellie rubbed her forehead.

Maybe it was an inherited trait to believe that people came back from the dead. First Belinda, and now her mother.

In fact, June looked happier than she had before Ellie had told her, and Ellie's stomach sank down to her toes. Surely there wasn't any truth in the whole concept?

June composed her face and her voice was matter-of-fact. 'Does she, now? Well, that makes me feel a lot better,' she half mumbled to herself.

This was getting worse and worse. 'June?' Ellie could see enormous problems coming up when she couldn't share any of this with Luke. 'What do you know about Travis and the fact that they didn't find his body?'

June's face was innocent. Too innocent. 'Nothing, of course. I went to the memorial service. I'm just looking out for Belinda.'

Ellie sighed. She believed that part of it. A dull ache had started behind her eyes and she avoided the questions that were forming. She was too tired to cope with the Travis question at the moment. She'd deal with one problem at a time. She glanced at the clock and saw there was still half an hour before she had to get ready.

'I believe you should tell Belinda you're her mother. And you should do it *before* she has the baby.'

June twisted her head away from that thought. 'I'll think about it.'

Ellie had to bring out the big guns. 'Did you know that Mrs Farrell told Belinda that she's coming into the labour room when she has the baby?'

June's face reflected the horror of her worst fear.

Ellie hammered her point home. 'Belinda said she doesn't know how to stop her but she certainly doesn't want her there. But she could have her real mother to stand up for her and together you should be able to keep Elsa Farrell out.'

June bit her lip and Ellie felt really mean, pressuring the older woman, but they'd created such a coil. The euphoria of a birth was a wonderful chance to start fresh and new.

'Think about it, June. Belinda needs you to stand up beside her and give her strength.' She laid her hand on the other woman's fingers again. 'You must have been frightened when you had your baby, you would have liked to have your mother there. You can be there when Belinda most needs you.'

June's voice was whisper quiet and Ellie had to lean forward to catch the words. 'That woman was there when I had Belinda. She sat in the corner like a vulture and I can still remember seeing her cold face as I screamed with the pain.' She shuddered.

Ellie shivered at the trickle of ice that had run down her spine. Elsa Farrell was a bad person.

Poor June. The midwife in Ellie wanted to strangle Luke's mother. But all she said was, 'Then I'm sure you understand why Belinda doesn't want her there.'

June nodded.

Ellie took her hand away and finished dryly, 'And if by some *miracle* Belinda's husband appears...' June looked away and Ellie just shook her head '...then you can run interference between them and the explosion that's going to hit like a nuclear blast from Elsa Farrell.' Let alone Luke, Ellie thought, and hoped she wouldn't get the blame because she was unwillingly privy to a part of the whole confusing fog.

June looked up and met Ellie's eyes. 'I'm sorry to drag you into all this, Ellie. But I had to tell someone and I will think about what you've said.' She stood up. 'I'd better go. You have to go to work and I've taken up too much of your time already.' She handed Ellie a scrap of paper. 'If you need to contact me, this is my address and phone number.'

'Thank you for thinking I can be trusted with your confidences.' She took the paper, folded it and slipped it in her purse. 'I'm sure you'll do the right thing. But Belinda needs you now, not later.'

June nodded and moved towards the door. 'I do feel better and I hope you have a good night at work.'

Ellie gave a strangled laugh. How on earth would she keep her mind on the job with all this running around inside her brain? 'Thank you. Goodnight, June.'

Ellie shut the door after her visitor and leaned back against it. She wished she could ring Luke and talk to him about it. June might feel better but Ellie certainly felt burdened with the knowledge that she was keeping Luke in the dark about Belinda's suspicions and June's strange reaction to the possibility that his brother, Travis, might be alive.

She pushed herself off the door and went to shower before work. Oh, goody. Another shift with Anthea could only add to her misery.

Friday night in the maternity ward was quiet. Ellie locked the door after the evening staff left and went into the nursery. Anthea wasn't talking to her, which wasn't too different but Ellie had too much on her mind to let it affect her tonight.

Summer Brown and her twins had gone home, as had Sue Carter and Harley, and Mavis Donahue was rooming in with her baby and didn't need any help.

That left Jackie Deverill's baby, Peter, in the nursery

as he was still having occasional slowing of his heart rate. To further complicate his first few days of life, he was now on nasogastric feeds because his jaundice had made him too sleepy to feed at the breast.

He was under the lights for forty-eight hours so Ellie at least had something to do in the nursery.

Anthea had disappeared into the office to attend to paperwork and Ellie was happy pottering around doing Peter's observations and making up milk mixtures to cover his extra fluid quota.

When a baby like Peter had to go under the phototherapy lights, his sweating from the radiant heat was initially more than he would usually drink. Extra formula was added to the colostrum his mother expressed three-hourly and which was put down the tube into his stomach.

Jackie would have to wait for her full milk to come in and for Peter to wake up enough to drink from the breast again. It would take two days or more probably before they could establish breastfeeding again when the baby's jaundice was resolved.

Ellie had finished the tube feed and because Peter was settled, Jackie had returned to bed. The monitor beeped constantly in time with Peter's heart rate and the nursery was peaceful. Unlike Ellie's thoughts.

Maybe she was going crazy, but June had practically confirmed that Travis could turn up for Belinda's baby's birth, or at least she knew more than she was letting on.

Ellie worried at her dilemma with Luke like a dog with a bone. She didn't think she could ever forgive Travis, if he were indeed found to be alive, for not including his brother in the deception—no matter what the reason. But, then, if Luke had been included, he would never have countenanced such an elaborate manipulation of people's emotions.

She heard the phone ringing in the office and a few minutes later Anthea came in and spoke to a spot over Ellie's left shoulder.

'Dr Farrell is sending his sister-in-law for admission via ambulance with a frontal headache and blurred vision. I've set up birthing because it's the room with the most emergency equipment, but I might need a hand if she fits.'

Ellie felt her throat go dry. 'She has had some oedema and slight hypertension. Hopefully Luke will be able to control her blood pressure with medication.'

'We'll see.' Anthea softened at Ellie's genuine distress. 'The poor girl had a hard time losing her husband like that, and now this.' She met Ellie's eyes. 'Because you know her better, would you prefer to look after her yourself and I can finish in the nursery?'

Ellie's jaw felt slack with shock and she tried to hide her surprise. 'That's very nice of you, I'd like that. Thank you, Anthea!'

'Yes, well,' Anthea drawled, 'you seem to be the flavour of the month.' And with that cryptic comment she went across to the office to shut the computer down and bring her things into the nursery.

Ellie didn't have time to dwell on Anthea's abrupt about-face—she just took advantage of it.

Ellie collected the most used drugs for hypertensive crisis, hydralazine and magnesium sulphate injections, an IV set-up and an adult heart monitor.

Belinda must have rung Luke. She might even have tried Ellie's place, too, but of course no one had been home there.

When the ambulance arrived, Anthea let them in and

Luke followed before Belinda had even been wheeled into the birthing suite.

Belinda smiled wanly up at Ellie as she lay on the trolley. 'I did ring when the bad headache came, like you said.'

Ellie stroked Belinda's cheek. 'Clever girl. Now, just relax and we'll have you feeling better soon.' Belinda closed her eyes and Ellie met Luke's look over the top of the trolley.

For once his hair was mussed and his tie was crooked, which was testimony to how serious he considered Belinda's condition.

They moved Belinda onto the labour bed and Ellie started a chart for Belinda's observations.

'What's her blood pressure?' Luke didn't look up as he inserted the intravenous cannula into Belinda's other arm.

'One-ninety over one twenty-five,' Ellie replied, with a worried look at the sphygmomanometer. Belinda's diastolic blood pressure was dangerously high for a pregnant mum and her baby.

'We'd better get it down, then.' He looked at the drugs Ellie had laid out on the trolley and selected the hydralazine. 'She's not too hyper-reflexive but we'll start the magnesium sulphate anyway. Hopefully, she won't need it.'

With pre-eclampsia the general rules for treatment were admission to hospital, bed rest and careful monitoring. Luke's aims were to prevent Belinda from having a seizure, lower her blood pressure, as the risk of stroke for the mother was real with very high blood pressure, and decide when to deliver the baby.

By the time Ellie's shift was over, Belinda's condition was stable.

Ellie made the day staff promise to call her if Belinda's condition worsened. She needed to see June to tell her that her daughter had been admitted during the night.

Luckily she'd put June's address in her purse and she didn't have to go home first to find it. When she pulled up outside the house number June had given her, the blinds were drawn and nobody seemed to be about.

It was a small, wooden house with a white picket fence that needed a coat of paint. A few straggly roses bloomed against the house wall and a dog barked behind the fence when Ellie knocked at the front door. An air of loneliness prevailed.

After a few moments Ellie could hear footsteps, and then June opened the door in her dressing-gown. Her face looked pale behind her black-rimmed glasses.

'Ellie? What's wrong?' She clutched the gown around herself tightly.

Ellie held her hands up helplessly. 'Can I come in, June?'

June stepped forward. 'Oh, of course.' She pushed open the screen door to allow Ellie past into the room. 'Sit down. Do you want a cup of tea?'

'No, thanks.' Ellie moved towards the lounge, sat down and patted the seat beside her. 'Sit for a minute, June.'

June's eyes widened. 'What's happened? Is Belinda all right?'

'That's why I'm here. But, yes, she's all right. Now.'

June started to ask what had happened and Ellie put up her hand. 'It might be easier if you let me give you the facts and you can ask questions when I'm finished. Is that OK?'

June bit her lip and nodded.

'Belinda has had a rise in her blood pressure over the last few weeks and last night her condition became worse.'

June gasped and Ellie patted her hand. 'She's OK. She rang Luke and he arranged for her to come into the hospital by ambulance. Her blood pressure has been controlled quite strongly by medications and she's stable now, but she won't be leaving hospital until after her baby is born.'

'Pre-eclampsia! I had pre-eclampsia but it didn't get too bad.' June took her glasses off and rubbed the lenses with her hanky as if unable to keep still.

'Belinda's hypertension was quite dangerous when she first came in but Luke seems to have it sorted now. Ideally he'd like to ensure Belinda is more stable before bringing on the baby's birth. But that will depend on how much the tablets can control it.

'If the medication can't settle her blood pressure, or if it goes up as high as it was last night, then Luke might consider a Caesarean section. Sometimes it's safer for mother and baby in a crisis. Do you understand?'

June's eyes were huge and she nodded. 'So we don't know when she's going to have the baby, or how it's going to be born yet?'

'That's right. But I would guess it won't be any longer than the next couple of days. The thing with this condition is that it doesn't really get any better until after the baby is born. There comes a time when the baby, even if it's a few weeks early, is safer out of his mum's tummy than in. And the mother is also at risk as long as the pregnancy continues.'

June bit her finger. 'So if her husband were alive, he'd

better get back here pronto.' She met Ellie's eyes and her voice was resolute. 'I have to ring Travis.'

Ellie felt like putting her hands over her ears, now she had finally discovered the truth about Travis's 'death'. She didn't want to hear this. 'I wouldn't know about that, June, but if I was her mother, I'd be sitting quietly with her at the hospital, being her friend.' The warning in Ellie's voice was unmistakable. 'And I'd be really careful of surprises while she's so unwell.'

'And keeping unwelcome people, like Elsa Farrell, away, too.' The resolution in June's voice was a new sound to Ellie.

'Perhaps,' Ellie said. 'The main thing is she's in a safe place, and people are looking out for her. But I think she's in need of a special, motherly friend.' They smiled at each other in perfect understanding.

'Thank you for coming to tell me, Ellie, otherwise I might not have found out until Monday morning.'

Ellie stood up. 'You're welcome.' But she was thinking that now June had stated she would ring Travis, Ellie had no excuse not to tell Luke the truth. She rubbed her forehead to ease the ache. 'I have to go home now to pick up my son. I'll probably see you at the hospital when I come up to visit Belinda.'

June followed her to the door. 'But she will be all right, won't she?'

'Luke will be watching her very closely. Don't worry.' Ellie kissed the woman's cheek. 'Bye, June.' To her surprise, June hugged her before opening the door.

Ellie shook her head as she walked down the path. 'Oh, what tangled webs we weave', she thought. Luke was never going to forgive her for not telling him about Travis, but she just couldn't. It wasn't her place to—it was Travis's.

CHAPTER TEN

Josh seemed almost energetic and Ellie lay around the house and watched him play with his cars. At eleven o'clock he came to Ellie as she dozed on the lounge and poked her. 'That man's outside the door.'

Ellie blinked and sat up. 'Thank you, darling.' She was sure she'd locked the screen door. She ran her fingers though her hair and the longer locks reminded her that her hair was growing.

It was indeed Luke. He looked great and for a moment Ellie just wanted to pour out all the information she had in her head and hear him say he'd sort it all out. But she couldn't, and she couldn't quite meet his eyes as guilt and confusion about her options warred with her undeniable pleasure in seeing him.

'Hello, Luke,' was all she said.

'Hello, Ellie. I hope I didn't wake you.'

Ellie unlocked the door so that he could come in. 'I've been doing that gross half-asleep-lie-around-in-a-stupor thing that happens after night duty if you don't go to bed. So a visit is fine.'

He stopped at the lounge-room door and smiled at Josh. 'Hello, Josh. Remember me?'

Josh nodded. 'Thank you for my cars. I have a picture for you.' He picked himself off the floor and went off to his bedroom.

'He loves the cars.' Ellie slid past Luke, careful not to touch him, and sat down on one end of the lounge.

Luke sat on the chair opposite and drank in the sight

of her. She looked weary and even a little stressed, which was something he didn't associate with Ellie.

'Everything all right with you, Ellie?'

She avoided his eyes and he could have sworn she'd jumped when he'd asked that.

'Fine. I'm just tired. I probably need some exercise. What can I do for you, Luke?'

Except for a puckered frown on her forehead, her face was expressionless and he felt like he was standing on the other side of a glass window and couldn't reach her. It drove him crazy that she wouldn't let him in. Something was going on and he wanted to smooth the worry from her brow.

'Don't shut me out, Ellie. I want to be here for you. I want to be here for both you and Josh.'

This time she did jump. 'I'm not your responsibility and neither is my son.'

That hurt. It was painfully true that Josh wasn't his son and Luke had to force back the urge to shout that he wished he *was* Josh's father. That he should have been, in fact.

She wouldn't meet his eyes and Luke could tell that now wasn't a good time to go down that road and start another row. He relaxed his shoulders and breathed out slowly.

Josh walked back into the room and Luke was glad of the diversion. The boy handed Luke a stick picture of himself with big muscles, playing with a car. The drawing made Luke smile, which helped. 'Thank you, Josh. It's a great picture.' He pointed to the car. 'Is that one of your new cars?'

Josh nodded and climbed up onto the lounge to lean on his mother. His thin little legs were tucked up under him and Luke wanted to take them both in his arms and protect them from the world. But he knew he'd have to be patient.

'I came to ask if you would both like to come to the beach with me. I've got a picnic.' He watched Josh's face light up. 'I'm going to the cove and I even found an old bucket and spade for Josh, if he doesn't have one, for building sandcastles.'

Ellie closed her eyes. This was exactly what she didn't want—the cove and all its memories. The two of them, on the beach together, with Luke offering to share her concerns. It would be so easy to give in and let him take over her life—but what would be left of her soul if she gave up her independence and then lost him?

Uncomfortably, she squirmed under the nagging guilt about all those secrets between them.

Ellie started to say, 'I don't think—'

In his excitement, Josh cut her off. 'Please, Mummy. Can we go to the beach? We haven't been for ages.'

More guilt! Ellie knew that was true. When they'd moved up here she'd promised Josh they'd go the beach nearly every day, and since she'd started work there just hadn't been the time. Plus, she was worried about Josh's health. Maybe he needed more sunshine and exercise. She sighed and dropped a kiss on his hair. 'OK, sweetheart. If that's what you'd like to do.'

She narrowed her eyes at Luke. He wasn't playing fair to offer a treat like that in front of Josh. 'Let's go and eat Dr Farrell's food and Mummy can sleep on the beach while you and Dr Farrell build sandcastles.' Serve him right. Luke just grinned back.

Ellie dragged herself to her feet, slightly exaggerating her tiredness in the scant hope that Luke would feel guilty for making her do something she didn't want to do. But he didn't look repentant. She gave up and searched out some towels, a bottle of juice and sunscreen. She even grabbed a pillow and a hat for putting over her eyes as she slept in case he thought she was joking.

Luke eyed the large pile of extras that mounted by the front door. 'You might have to help me put these in the car, Josh. I think your mother wants to spend the night at the beach.'

Josh shouted with joy. 'Can we, Mum? Can we?'

'Dr Farrell was joking.' Josh's mouth turned down and Ellie was pleased to see that Luke looked crestfallen that he'd built up the boy's hopes. She bit her lip to stop smiling. Perfect.

As Luke carried the last of the stuff out to the car with Josh, Ellie tilted her head. 'What about Belinda?'

Luke patted his pocket. 'I've just come from the hospital. She's resting quietly and I have my mobile phone if they need me. But I think we have the situation under control for the moment.'

Ellie nodded. She did have faith in Luke's diagnostics, but, then, she had faith in Luke's everything. Even his mother was predictably horrible.

When they arrived at the cove, there was no one else there. A rock pool had filled with seawater from the last tide and Josh happily played in the ankle-deep water while Ellie set her towel down on a patch of sand near him.

Luke had produced a bucket and spade and even a couple of plastic boats. They looked suspiciously new to Ellie but she didn't say anything as he put them down beside Josh.

Ellie plumped up her pillow and pulled her hat down over her eyes. 'Well, enjoy the water, gentlemen. I'm having a doze and Dr Farrell is in charge of public safety.' She lay down under the umbrella that Luke had brought and smiled. This wasn't so bad after all.

When she woke later, Ellie was stiff and she noticed that the umbrella angle had been changed to protect her as the sun had moved. Josh and Luke were walking along the edge of the waves, facing away from her.

She stood up to stretch the kinks out of her back, and although she'd decided not to visit the cave, the pull was too strong. She'd be back before Luke and Josh returned. She just wanted to see what she remembered about it.

She scrambled up past the coarse grass that protected the overhang from curious eyes on the beach below. To call it a cave was glorifying it, but the overhanging rock did shelter the sandy floor from the weather. Ellie stepped inside and the air seemed cooler in the dimness. The distant memories flooded back.

They'd been so young and idealistic. So sure they could just set a date for five years' time and nothing would go wrong before they met again to take up their lives together. She gave a half-laugh.

She felt an echo of that bubbling excitement she'd had when she'd decided to ask Luke to make love to her before she left, so that she could take a part of him with her. Not a baby, but an imprint on her heart and soul that she would never lose. But he'd refused.

How life changed people. She'd been a wife and a mother since that time, and she'd thought it would never be the same between them. But the magic was still there—she couldn't deny that, no matter how frightened she was.

'I thought I'd find you here,' Luke said. A gull screamed overhead and the breeze billowed open his shirt as she swung around.

He was alone, and for a mad moment it was as if she

were seventeen again and he'd come to sweep her into his arms and she could be his. But in the same moment Ellie remembered Josh on the beach, unsupervised. He saw her eyes widen and forestalled her question.

'There's another family down there now. I know them well and Josh is with their children. I'd make sure he was safe, Ellie.' There was some censure in his voice for her thoughts and she nodded. Of course he would.

She looked around the cave to avoid his eyes. 'Have you been back here much in the last ten years?'

He looked up at the ceiling of the overhang and the heart he'd scaped out was still there. They could still read the letters inside the heart. 'Not once.'

Suddenly it was too hard to stay apart. She stepped into his arms and he just held her against his body. The scent of her filled his nostrils and she fitted into his body like no one else ever had. He stood there silently, thinking about that day all those years ago and what had happened in between.

Ellie McGuire had blown into his life during that Christmas break, as unexpected as she'd been miraculous. After only a month she'd felt so heart breakingly right for him. A free-spirited sea nymph with a joy of life the like of which he'd never seen before, certainly not in his parents' emotionally sterile house.

He'd wanted to carry his Ellie off to a tower and keep her there until he could provide for them both. But she'd been right. They'd both been too young and they'd both had dreams.

It had been as if she had been twenty-two and he the seventeen-year-old.

He could remember saying, 'Promise you'll come back and marry me. I'll wait five years for you. You should be able to finish your nursing, do your midwifery and what ever else you want by then, and we'll set up practice together.' He'd worked it out.

He remembered when she'd reached up and kissed his lips. 'I won't promise I'll marry you, but I will contact you in five years.' But she hadn't come back.

Ellie lifted her gaze to the heart Luke had engraved on the ceiling and then her lashes came down to shield her eyes. He heard her sigh. 'It was a lovely teen romance,' she said, and he could hear the finality in her voice. But he wasn't giving up.

He shook his head. 'It had potential. Still has enormous potential—now more than ever as we're both fully grown up. If one of the people involved would stop being so stubborn.'

Not stubborn, deathly frightened, Ellie thought. But she didn't say it. 'We've both changed.'

'As we should.' Luke's voice was firm. 'Ten years is a long time and I find the mature woman even more fascinating than the girl I fell in love with. I will always love you, Ellie.'

She shook her head in denial. 'Always is a long time— especially if one of us is gone.' Her fear showed in her eyes and it was as if a great weight had been lifted off his shoulders. Finally he realised why she wouldn't let him closer.

Luke tried to control the surge of excitement his understanding had brought. He had to be careful. 'I'm not going to leave you like Steve did.' He felt her shudder at the thought and his arms tightened. His head came down to hers and he tasted the salt from her tears. He had to convince her.

He crouched a little so that his eyes were level with hers. 'You're safe with me, Ellie.' He could see himself reflected in her eyes but she still shook her head.

He squeezed her against him gently and then loosened his hold.

'Can't you give us a chance? You could even live with me if you didn't want to get married again.' He smiled into her eyes. 'Of course I'd prefer the legal option but I've waited too long for you to risk it all for something you might never be ready for.'

She looked at this man who could give her everything she needed. He offered her stability for Josh, a feeling that she belonged somewhere and most of all a love that was strong and true.

Maybe if she lived with him she wouldn't feel so insecure about being good enough for him. Helped by Elsa Farrell's contempt, that feeling she had that socially she was unacceptable was just another barrier she was using to keep him at arm's length. She knew deep in herself that Luke couldn't have cared less for society's comment on the woman he wanted as his partner.

If she lived with him and it didn't work out, then he wouldn't be saddled with a wife that didn't fit in. The concept was too big so she concentrated on the trivia. 'That's a pretty brave offer for a conservative guy in a small town.'

'See the lengths I'd go to to keep you.' Luke kissed her hair and she smelt like herbal shampoo and sea salt and a whiff of acquiescence that he hoped he hadn't misread. A serpent of desire coiled deep in his gut and he stared at her as he fought the urge to take her, as she'd wanted him to do all those years ago—and he hadn't.

Fool. He should have branded her his when he'd the chance. He'd lusted after her from the first moment he'd seen her frolic in the waves in his deserted cove but his fear of consequences had won when she'd offered herself that last night before she'd left.

She stood in front of him now, like an oasis to drink from, and in his desert of a life he'd never wanted to sip more.

He brushed her shoulders, and her skin felt like gold satin under his fingers, then down and across the hollow of her stomach, and she shuddered beneath his touch. Her eyes seemed to shimmer like phosphorus in the ocean in the muted light of the sandstone overhang, and he felt as though he was falling down a swirling whirlpool, with Ellie the siren beckoning him deeper.

He kissed her hair and then her cheeks and the tip of her nose. 'Kiss me, for all the years that we lost between, Ellie.'

His lips hovered a breath away from hers and Ellie closed her eyes. She wanted to feel his mouth on hers so badly, and if she kissed him it didn't mean she'd agreed. In the end, nothing could have prevented her final sway to meet him.

Ephemeral at first, she touched his mouth with hers and then they were joined—soft and gentle rubbings and murmurs—and then a more definite staking of his claim by Luke that took their journey into a more potent realm.

For a moment she sensed him hover on the edge of control before he leashed himself and gentled his mouth. A wanton, wicked part of her wanted to drive him over the edge to see what lay below the surface of that restraint. She suspected that was a side of him that only she could release. But she didn't and he groaned as he pulled away. She couldn't deny that this was where she belonged. Nothing had ever felt as right as this. Nothing ever would.

Ellie wrapped her arms across her chest to quell the tiny tremors that still reverberated and she stepped away. She couldn't do this now. There were too many secrets between them. But soon she would have to decide. If only she could have stood before him with a clean slate—with no secrets. And she had to think about her son in this equation, for she wasn't the only vulnerable one in this situation. 'I want to go back to Josh.'

He gave her a thoughtful look and then sighed. He brushed her cheek with his finger and took her hand. 'I won't be patient for ever. But for the moment I'll wait. Let's go.'

They tore Josh away from his new friends and re-packed the car. Both Ellie and Luke were quiet—which was lucky as Josh was chatting away about his exciting afternoon. Luke didn't stay when he dropped them off at Ellie's house but she knew he considered the unfinished business between them untenable. The clock was ticking until he'd had enough.

Ellie didn't hear from Luke on Sunday or even see him at the hospital when she visited Belinda on Sunday evening.

Belinda's eyes were shining and impatiently she urged Ellie to sit down beside the bed.

'Did you know that June has been visiting me a couple of times a day since I was admitted?'

Ellie nodded, guessing what was to come.

Belinda leant across and whispered in Ellie's ear, 'I said I wished she was my mum and suddenly she told me.' Belinda sat back and hugged herself. 'She said, "I hope you're not too disappointed?"' Belinda shook her head incredulously at the concept of being disappointed.

'June is my natural mother,' she said again.

Ellie felt the tears prickle at the pure joy in Belinda's face. Thank goodness June had finally beaten her demons.

'That's wonderful news, Belinda.'

'Isn't it? I have my own mother. And my baby will have a real grandmother—not just that horrible Mrs Farrell.' Belinda sighed back against her pillows. 'And she's promised she won't let Travis's mum into the room when I'm having my baby.'

'That's great,' Ellie said, but privately she wondered how June would be able to stop the woman.

'She's spoiling me but I just feel so comfortable with her. I want her with me when I go into labour. Now I'll have two people with me. I'm thinking of telling her about that other matter I discussed with you.' Her eyes darted around the room as if someone might be listening. 'What do you think?'

Ellie didn't quite meet Belinda's eyes. 'I think June could be a good person to have on your side. I'm sure anything you tell her won't go any further.'

Belinda nodded, satisfied. 'That's what I thought.'

Ellie gathered her bag and keys. 'Have you told Luke about June being your mother?'

Belinda shook her head. 'I haven't told anybody else yet. I just want to hug it to myself for a while. But I will.'

Ellie sighed. Soon that would be one less secret between her and Luke. She didn't think she could stand the suspense much longer. 'I have to go. I dropped Josh at the Judds' while I came in here. I'll come up to visit you after work tomorrow.'

'When do you think I'll have my baby, Ellie?'

Ellie spread her hands. 'That really depends on how your blood pressure goes and the blood tests that Luke is ordering for you every second day.'

She smiled and jiggled her keys. 'You might even go into labour naturally because if your body thinks it's time for your baby to be born then that's what happens.' She dropped a kiss on Belinda's cheek and stood up. 'But at a guess, because you've settled down so well, Luke would be looking at inducing your labour late in the week.'

'So by next weekend I'll be a mother.'

'That's my guess. See you tomorrow.' Belinda nodded but there was a dreamy look on her face as she contemplated finally holding her baby in her arms. Ellie prayed that all would go well.

During Monday and Tuesday a strained truce existed between Ellie and Luke at the surgery.

On Wednesday, Ellie took Josh for his blood tests at lunchtime and she marvelled at the little boy's stoicism when the pathology technician took his blood. A sudden, horrible thought crossed her mind but it was too terrible to contemplate. Steve had had that same stoicism during his treatment for leukaemia. Ellie shuddered and banished the comparison as far from her mind as possible. She refused to think like that or she'd be a basket case by Friday. Her son was tired and had probably picked up some viral illness.

Back at work, the afternoon became a steady stream of clients and minor procedures for Ellie, and she was glad to be occupied with work.

At the end of the day, Luke leaned on the doorframe of Ellie's room and dropped his suggestion as if it were a *fait accompli*.

'What time do you want me to pick you up to go to the Hollowses' dinner party tonight?'

Ellie's eyes widened. She'd forgotten about that, although she'd arranged babysitting with Lil last week. She rubbed her forehead and considered cancelling. Then she realised what Luke had said. 'Since when was I going to the Hollow's with you?'

'Louise rang me and asked if I could pick you up. I thought you knew.' He shrugged. 'If you want to take your car, that's fine, but as we're both going I thought it seemed a sensible idea.'

'I don't think I'll be going.' There, she'd said it. So why did she feel so depressed?

Luke stared at her. 'Why don't you want to go? I thought you liked Louise?'

Ellie licked her lips at the accusing tone, and her voice wasn't as confident as she would have liked it to be.

'I'm worried about Josh and I don't think I should leave him with Mrs Judd when he's not well.'

Luke's voice softened. 'I'm sorry. I should have realised.' He stepped into the room and tucked his finger under Ellie's chin until she couldn't avoid his eyes. 'Isn't Josh asleep by seven-thirty?'

Ellie nodded. 'But it still doesn't feel right.'

'You should get out more, Ellie, and think about your own happiness for a change. Besides, I'd like you to come with me. How about we go for a short time? You can leave the Hollow's phone number with Mrs Judd, and if she has any concerns with Josh then she can ring and I'll bring you straight home.'

Ellie wavered, and against her instincts she nodded.

'Why would Louise think you'd want to take me?' Ellie was going to have a few words to say to Louise.

He stroked her cheek and his voice dropped. 'Since I told her that I had decided to pursue an old flame with a view to long-term commitment.'

Ellie held her ground but couldn't help the warmth in her stomach his words created. 'Old flame, eh?' She tilted her head. 'How old would this flame be?'

His eyes narrowed dangerously. 'Old enough to know better than to flirt with danger in an empty building. I would suggest you shut down your computer and go home to change. I'll pick you up at seven-thirty once you've settled Josh.' He spun on his heel and returned to his room. His tone had bite in it. Luke was as churned up as she was. Ellie hugged that thought to herself. He'd always been so controlled.

Ellie's heart thumped and, despite her uneasiness about leaving Josh, she couldn't help acknowledge an excitement about the coming evening. Ellie stared at the empty space where he'd been. She must have stood there for a couple of minutes because Luke's voice echoed down the hallway.

'Ellie? If you don't leave now I'll have to demonstrate how tired I'm getting of all this procrastination.'

Ellie jumped and switched off her computer. She grabbed her bag and moved to the door of her room. To her own disgust she peered up the hallway to see that Luke was nowhere in sight before slipping out the door.

'See you at seven-thirty,' she said as she pulled the outside door shut behind her.

CHAPTER ELEVEN

LOUISE HOLLOWS'S house was set on five acres of cliff-top that fell away to the sea. The fact that Louise had a gardener was very apparent. To maintain the shrubbery and flower-beds would be a full-time job, and the scent from the red roses lining the long driveway drifted into the car as Luke drove Ellie up to the front portico. 'It's beautiful,' Ellie gulped.

'Hop out and I'll park the car,' he said.

Ellie reluctantly opened her door. 'I'll wait here for you. This is all a lot grander than I had imagined.' She glanced down at her simple black dress.

Luke must have picked up her reservations because before he drove off he took the time to reassure her. 'You look wonderful.'

She saw his teeth flash as he grinned. 'And Louise and her husband are the same sexually frustrated people you told to "get stuck into it".'

Very funny, Ellie felt like saying, but she was just too nervous. She hoped that piece of antenatal advice didn't come up over the dinner table talk.

Luke drove up the drive a little further and into a square that held several other expensive-looking cars. Some little dinner party, Ellie thought morosely. This was partly why she couldn't marry Luke. She'd never fit into the social scene. Luke should have a polished wife like Anthea, not a drifter like Ellie.

The crash and tumble of the waves floated up from the cliffs below and the sea breeze tickled Ellie's neck. As the last of the sunlight faded, Ellie walked very slowly towards the imposing front steps and waited at the bottom for Luke to catch her up.

When Luke appeared beside her, it was comforting to feel his hand on her elbow. He looked fabulous in black trousers and jacket with a round-necked black shirt underneath. He seemed so different tonight and that was adding to Ellie's nervousness.

Then Louise was at the door. She greeted Ellie like her long-lost sister, and for a heavily pregnant woman she still managed to practically drag Ellie in to meet the rest of the couples. Ellie turned her head back towards Luke as if to ask for help, but he was watching her with a half-smile on his face.

'Everyone.' She gestured grandly. 'This is Ellie Diamond. Ellie's been back in town only a month, and she's working three days a week for Luke.'

Louise's husband came up and shook Ellie's hand and passed her a champagne flute. 'I'm Ben.' He grinned wickedly and Ellie blushed. 'Welcome, Ellie.'

An older couple came up and the woman's face was filled with warmth. 'So you're Ellie. My son and daughter-in-law haven't stopped raving about you since they had their baby and you looked after them—Mavis and John Donahue.'

Ellie smile back in relief. 'They were fabulous. And your grandson is gorgeous, Mrs Donahue.'

'You must have been pretty fabulous yourself. I can't believe you convinced John to cut the cord.'

Her husband chimed in. 'Or sit in the bathroom, rubbing Mavis's back for all that time.'

Ellie smiled. 'He's a very proud dad.'

Another couple introduced themselves and had also heard of Ellie through relatives who'd had a baby.

Then a small, dark-haired woman appeared and there was something familiar about the woman's face. 'Hi. I'm Susan. We met when you decided to dress "corporate" for Luke.'

Ellie placed her. 'I remember. It's lovely to see you again.'

Luke appeared at her elbow and her smile wasn't as strained as it had been earlier. 'Everyone is so friendly, I'm feeling better.'

He slid an arm around her and squeezed her shoulder. A few people looked and smiled at Luke's gesture. 'They are all genuine people. You fit in perfectly.'

'Was it that obvious I was nervous?' The warmth from Luke's arm seaped into her and it felt too good to slip out from under. 'So long as these people or their relatives keep having babies, we'll have something to talk about.'

'I've never found your conversation boring, I don't see why anyone else would.' He squeezed her shoulder again and the goose-bumps ran down her arms. Ellie sipped her drink to distract herself. He lowered his head and his voice. 'Did I ever tell you that I think you have the sexiest voice in the whole world?'

Ellie spluttered a little into her drink. 'Now who's flirting?'

He just smiled and steered her across the room. 'Come and see the patio. The lights in the pool area are pretty special.'

As they went out onto the patio they could see strings of fairy lights that ran in different directions, like spokes from a wheel, and hidden lights bathed a waterfall at one end of the pool.

'It's incredible.' Ellie leant on the rail and Luke came to stand behind her with one hand on either side of her.

She could feel his body against her. It was just too tempting not to lean back into him.

His voice rumbled in her hair. 'You are incredible.'

There was silence for a minute and then he leaned more firmly against her and wrapped his arms around her. Ellie felt safe and warm and a slow burn had started low in her stomach. She couldn't resist a tiny slide of her bottom from side to side against his thighs and he leant down and nibbled her ear. 'After this party is over we have to have a serious discussion about our future together.' Luke's voice was deep and low and thrummed against her neck. 'I've waited too long for this,' he said.

He stepped back and let his arms fall away and she missed the firmness of his body with an ache. Then his shoulder rubbed against hers as he leant over the rail beside her. 'I may have to stand here for a while. Someone appears to have excited me into a state that's not publicly acceptable.'

'Now, who would that be?' Ellie put her hand into his and squeezed his fingers.

Louise appeared at the door. 'Entrées are being served, you two.'

'Should I tell Louise?' Luke teased.

'Tell me what?' Louise tilted her head. 'I can see you guys aren't quite ready to come in so I'll see you when you're ready.'

Ellie and Luke smiled secretly at each other and a few minutes later Luke ushered her to the table. Ellie felt cosseted by his care and she realised it could be addictive.

The way his warm gaze kept brushing her was affecting Ellie's appetite. It seemed that the few times she did put something to her mouth Luke was watching, until she found herself glancing at him before her food touched her lips.

His sleeve would touch her arm, his elbow brushed her side and Ellie felt the tautness inside her coil and intensify with every touch and glance between them.

The conversation flowed easily among the guests and to Ellie's surprise her occasional contributions were appreciated and she became even more relaxed.

Luke watched her with satisfaction. He'd come to a decision. Ellie was what he wanted and he would wait no longer. And the primitive pull that she exerted on him had reached the point where he had to act or go mad.

He would treat her like the mature woman she was. That had been his problem. She was younger than him but she was no child.

Look what had happened last time he'd backed off.

He wasn't willing to risk losing her for another ten years because of her own insecurities—or his.

They were the first guests to leave, and alone in the car with Luke on the way to her house, Ellie stole a glance at his profile. The nerves she had suffered on the way to the party were nothing compared to the trepidation she experienced as they drew closer to home. She wished he would just smile at her.

They pulled up outside her house and she glanced across at him again. 'Are you coming in?'

He gave a short, humourless laugh and turned to face her. His eyes met hers with an intensity that started the tremors in her arms again.

'I believe so,' he said. 'Wait. I'll get your door.'

So she sat there in the dark and listened to the crunch of his feet in the gravel as he walked around the car, and vacillated between capitulation and flight. She knew that he wanted a commitment from her and didn't think she had the strength to deny him. The car door opened and he handed her out as if she was something precious that needed protecting from the world, and she knew that if everything was perfect she could get used to that.

The tension stayed while she thanked Lil and saw her out. Luke came with Ellie while she checked on Josh, as if he was unwilling to let her out of his sight, and then there was nothing to do but to make her decision.

She smiled tremulously at him. 'I'm frightened that something is going to happen to spoil everything.'

'Nothing is going to happen that we can't control by being together.'

His words should have reassured her but a cold shiver crossed her neck and her eyes widened. Suddenly she needed to feel his arms around her and lose herself before all her fears came crashing in on her. 'Take me to bed, Luke. I need you with me.'

He crushed her against him exultantly and lifted her into his arms. 'You only have to ask…'

She lay against his chest in haze of lust and loneliness that had finally promised to lift, if only for one night.

He stopped as they went through the bedroom door and closed it behind them, and she knew there was no turning back. She remembered the last time they'd nearly made love and she'd been the one to stop it. He put her down and they swayed together.

She looked at him, achingly, as he leaned against the door, and the bedside light cast an orange light around the room and across his hips. Slowly, and together, they removed their clothes and then she was falling onto the bed wrapped in Luke's arms.

It was all she'd dreamed of and more. Luke's scent and warmth surrounded her. His hardness against her, his skin on hers, his mouth on her throat. For a half-lucid moment she wished she could watch from the ceiling to keep these memories with her for ever.

When he entered her it was as if she'd never been with another man, never born a child, had been waiting for him and only him. She cried out as she wrapped her legs around him and wept with the beauty of it. It was as she'd feared. She loved him and she would never be whole without him again.

Afterwards, he sighed her name and gathered her close to his side as he stroked her hair.

'This is only the beginning, and I'm not going to let you go again,' he said, and she believed him.

Belinda went spontaneously into labour at six o'clock on Thursday morning. Sam from Maternity rang Luke's mobile phone and Ellie jumped when it went off beside her bed.

Before she could reach for it, a showered and dressed Luke appeared from the bathroom and picked it up.

His smile was reassuring as he answered the call. Ellie tucked the sheet under her chin and hoped Josh would sleep in as usual.

Luke severed the call and sat down on the bed beside Ellie. 'Belinda's in labour. And her blood pressure's stable.'

His eyes twinkled. 'They're going to ring you as Belinda wants you to be there, too.'

'I'll be right behind you.' Ellie dashed towards the bathroom, her mind filled with questions about Belinda's labour. She almost didn't hear Luke's comment as he left.

'And I'll be right behind you just as soon as you realise it's where I belong.'

By the time Ellie arrived, June was there as well, and Luke smiled as Belinda kept calling June 'Mum'.

He raised an eyebrow at Ellie and lowered his voice so that the other two in the room couldn't hear. 'Did you know about this before?'

Ellie nodded and Luke's eyes narrowed for a moment before he shrugged. 'I've known them both a lot longer than you—didn't you think I should know?'

Ellie nodded again but hesitated to lay the blame on June and Belinda. After another searching look at Ellie, he shrugged at her lack of answer. 'Anyway, I think it's great.'

He raised his voice. 'Good luck, ladies. I'll be in contact with the ward between my theatre cases.' He glanced at Ellie and she winced at the puzzlement in his gaze as he left. Soon this would all be over and everything would be out in the open.

Then Elsa Farrell arrived. Ellie never figured out how Luke's mother had discovered that the baby was on its way, but it was too late now.

Ellie sighed and prepared for battle, but it was June who barred the woman's entrance to the room.

'I'd like to see you outside, Mrs Farrell.'

Elsa's eyes flashed. 'Not now, June.' She attempted to brush past and June planted herself in front of her.

'Now!' June said, and she took the older woman's arm and steered her into the relatives' waiting room.

Ellie and Belinda exchanged looks and Ellie resisted the temptation to move closer to the outside door to hear what was being said.

'Leave them to it. Let's get you into the shower, Belinda.' Ellie helped the young woman to stand, and by the time she was sitting on the ball in the bathroom June was back.

Two bright spots of colour rode in June's cheeks but she held her head high and there was no doubt who the victor had been. 'She's gone, and she's not coming back until after the baby is born.' She looked a little shame-faced. 'I should have done *that* years ago.'

'How *did* you do that?' Ellie couldn't help the question, and she glanced across at Belinda who was resting with her eyes closed.

June grunted. 'I said I'd tell everyone she had an affair with Belinda's father while her husband was alive. What she did to Belinda and me was because she was jealous I'd had his child.'

Ellie bit her lip to stop the quiver of amusement that would have been quite inappropriate in the face of June's ferocity.

Another contraction started and Ellie swapped back-rubbing places with June. 'I'll get some ice for Belinda to suck.' She smiled warmly at June in congratulations.

By midday, Belinda was deep in established labour. She'd passed the halfway mark and was half dozing between contractions and sighing loudly as she worked through them.

Her blood pressure had only crept up a little but if it went up much further Luke had ordered an epidural to help bring it down again. Belinda was against the idea.

At three in the afternoon, Belinda's progress was slow yet she was determined. 'I want to do this naturally. Travis would want me to do this without drugs and I'm going to,' she panted.

Ellie nodded and June's colour was leaching from her face as Belinda became more distressed. 'How much longer?' June whispered, and Ellie shook her head.

Belinda's dilation had halted and Ellie worried she wasn't headed for a failure to progress—the same problem that had caused Mavis's first baby to be a Caesarean delivery.

Ellie stroked the girl's knee. 'Belinda, I get the feeling you're holding back. Let it happen. Your baby wants to be born and you have to let go.'

Belinda's eyes filled with tears. 'But Travis isn't here. I was sure he would come.'

'I know, sweetheart, but the baby doesn't want to wait.'

'He has to come.' Belinda turned tortured eyes to her friend and Ellie felt the sting of emotion in her throat, too.

Ellie leaned across and put the tiny foetal Doppler against Belinda's abdomen. The baby's heart rate was gradually slowing and the longer the labour continued, the more tired the baby would get. This time the clip-clops of the infant's heartbeats weren't much faster than Belinda's heart rate. Ellie would have to call Luke.

A choking sound at the door made them all turn, and a bearded stranger stood there. Travel-stained and weary, he had tears in his eyes. 'I'm here, baby. I'm so sorry it took me so long.'

Belinda stood up from the shower, brushed past Ellie, nearly knocked June off her seat and stepped into his arms. She pressed her wet belly against his trousers and hung on for dear life.

'I knew you would come. You said you would come.' And then she burst into tears. As she sobbed the stiffness fell from her shoulders and Ellie reached across and turned off the hand shower. As she watched, Belinda swayed into the next pain as if she'd waited for it, even welcomed it.

The sound of her breathing changed and Ellie knew the baby's time was near. But she dreaded ringing Luke. How did she tell him his brother was alive and that she, Ellie, had known? It was even worse now that they had made love, and she could almost feel the sword above her head.

In the end she didn't have to ring him. Luke came anyway and the scene must have been hard to fathom in the frozen tableau in the bathroom. But Belinda's baby wouldn't wait, and even a resurrected brother couldn't interfere with the natural course of events. At six minutes past four on Thursday afternoon, Amelia June Farrell was born.

Afterwards, with Belinda's baby daughter snuggled against her mother's breasts and Travis gazing adoringly at his family, Luke shook his head as he tried to make sense of this new situation.

He looked at Ellie and his eyes narrowed at her lack of surprise. She could see the suspicion grow as he worked it out, and a hard knot of impending doom gathered in her stomach.

Ellie wanted to pull his head down on her breast and protect him from the fact that his brother hadn't told him. To say that she was sorry she hadn't been able to warn him. But it was too late for that.

'You knew?' His voice was full of incredulity and then disgust at her betrayal. 'How much more do you know that you didn't see fit to tell me?'

What could she say? There had been far too many secrets already. She nodded. 'I knew.'

His voice was loaded with contempt and Ellie flinched. 'How could you allow my grief, my mother's grief, to continue?' Ellie wanted to defend herself, but he cut her off.

'You knew I loved you and yet you didn't trust me enough to share this with me. Well, I have loyalties, even if you don't. Anthea was right. You are different to the rest of us. I don't think I could spend my life with someone who doesn't trust anyone. You'd condone it, wouldn't you? You believe in running away when things become too hard—trained by your mother, no doubt!'

Ellie's eyes flashed. 'I wouldn't start on about mothers, if I were you.'

At that his eyes flared again. 'Well, mine isn't going to suffer any longer than she has to. Travis!' His brother looked up from adoring his baby. 'We need to see Mother, now! I'll wait for you at the nurse's station.' He cast a final look of loathing at Ellie and stormed out the door.

June put her arm around Ellie as they stood beside Belinda's bed. June's arm was the only warm thing on Ellie's body. She felt as if a block of ice was wedged in her chest.

'It's just the first shock talking,' June said. 'He's not a man to hold a grudge.'

Ellie gave a strangled laugh but the tears behind the sound were clear. 'It's a little more than a grudge.'

'There are a lot more people in the secret than just you, and you only had a late warning. That's a fact Luke should cotton onto once he's over his grief and anger. Give him time, Ellie.'

Ellie nodded. She didn't believe her, though. 'Thank you, June.' Ellie looked across at the bed. 'Congratulations on your granddaughter.' June grinned in delight and Belinda smiled mistily at her mother.

June leaned up to kiss Ellie. 'I should have told Belinda a long time ago. I'm so glad you urged me to tell her before the baby was born.'

She held her hand out to Belinda and her daughter took it without hesitation.

Belinda shook her head. 'I think you're both wonderful. I've got a friend, a husband and a mother, and Amelia has a father and a grandmother. What more could I want?'

Ellie knew what *she* wanted, and that was to get out of there. She left them to catch up on all things they had to say. 'The evening staff will help Belinda get settled in her new room. I have to go home to Josh. I'm working tonight.' She patted the baby's cheek, and dropped a kiss on Belinda's. 'You were wonderful. I'll see you later when I come to work.' She smiled wanly. 'Your baby is gorgeous and I'm so glad Travis made it.'

When she left the room, Ellie pulled a handkerchief from her pocket and blew her nose. Well, that was that. Now, if only her own life would sort itself out.

Later, at home, Ellie felt as if she was trapped in a nightmare. She needed the sea breeze to blow away the tensions and emotions of the day.

As she helped Josh change into shorts, several small bruises on his legs caught her eye. She frowned. She hadn't noticed them yesterday. Sudden panic caused her to lift up his T-shirt and her blood chilled to see more finger shaped bruises down his back.

'Do you know how you made these bruises, Josh?'

Josh twisted to look at his legs and shook his head. 'I didn't fall over.'

All Ellie could see in her mind's eye was Steve before he died. He'd been pale like Josh and so easily bruised by the dysfunction in his blood from the leukaemia.

Ellie felt the bile rise in her throat and she pulled Josh close against her so that he couldn't see her distress. It had to be something else. She couldn't go through this again. She drew a shuddering breath and wondered where she would get the strength from.

This was retribution for not putting Josh first. Please,

God, don't take my little boy, she prayed silently. I'll never put him second again.

Wednesday's blood tests assumed enormous importance. Luke had ordered copies of the results to be sent directly to the paediatrician but Ellie was sure he would have been sent his own copy to be scanned into Josh's files. Except that Luke would be at the hospital till at least six, and he wouldn't be at the surgery to pick up the results.

Ellie bundled Josh into the car and raced around there. Of course, the surgery was shut. June was with Belinda. She drove on to the hospital and pulled up in the operating theatre car park.

When she burst into the outside office at Theatres, Luke was walking beside a stretcher, about to usher a new patient in. He took one look at her wild-eyed expression and gestured to the theatre nurse to wait. 'Excuse me for a few moments,' he said to the woman. He turned to Ellie. 'You'd better come into Sister's office.'

As soon as Ellie heard the door close behind Luke she turned on him. 'Look at Josh!' She slid the boy's shirt up and the bruises stood out like ink smudges on his pale skin. 'See what happens when I get sidetracked by you. I should have done something about this days ago. I need the results of his blood tests now. I can't wait until tomorrow.'

Luke crossed the room and pulled his chair right next to where Ellie was sitting with Josh on her lap.

He spoke to Josh. 'Hello, old man. You must be wondering why your mum is so upset.'

Josh nodded and Ellie gulped air past the lump in her throat as she stifled the sob that wanted to come out. Luke was right. She needed to be calm for Josh. But she'd panicked as all the implications had crashed in on her.

Luke was talking calmly to the child. 'Mums always get upset when their children get sick. So I'll try to get an appointment for this evening, if I can, so Mum doesn't have to wait until tomorrow for you to see the doctor.' Josh nodded and Ellie closed her eyes. That was sensible.

Luke picked up the phone and spoke to the paediatrician personally. He murmured something Ellie didn't hear and then agreed out loud. He put the phone down. 'He can get back to the hospital to meet you around seven o'clock. I'll come with you.'

Ellie's eyes flew open. She'd promised God she'd do this on her own. That way Josh would get well. 'I don't want you there. This is between Josh and I and the paediatrician.' She hugged her son and turned her shoulder to Luke. 'Josh is my responsibility and has nothing to do with you.' She knew she was being irrational but she was ready to bargain where the power was to keep her baby.

'Ellie? What I said this afternoon was in the heat of the moment. June explained—'

Ellie cut him off. 'I don't care about your problems. I just want Josh well.'

At seven o'clock that evening, the paediatrician was gravely troubled. 'We'll do further tests. My practice nurse is setting up for an urgent bone-marrow aspiration now, but I have to tell you, Mrs Diamond, it doesn't look good. We'll know more after some extra blood tests I want tonight, but we won't know anything definite until tomorrow. I'm very concerned about his blood-clotting time, which is why he's bruising so easily.'

Ellie nodded but her face felt frozen. 'What do you think it is?'

He hesitated and looked at Ellie over his glasses. 'I'd

give it a ninety per cent chance that your son has acute lymphocytic leukaemia.'

Ellie felt as if she were falling down a long black tunnel. She grasped at straws. 'And the other ten per cent?'

'Has your son had any viral infections lately?' The specialist's eyes were kind but Ellie had the feeling he was humouring someone with their head in the sand. Ellie tried to clear her mind and think back to before Josh had started to get tired. 'Just before we left Sydney he had a tummy bug, but he was well by the time we moved.'

He nodded and stood up. 'My nurse will be ready for us now. Are you going to stay with us while we do the procedure?'

Ellie squeezed Josh's hand. 'Of course.'

The next fifteen minutes were horrific for Ellie, and not much better for Josh. After a whimper as the local anaesthetic went in he just lay quietly on his stomach and let them syringe a sample of bone marrow and blood from his hip-bone. Ellie held his hand the whole time and the tears trickled down her face. Then they took venous blood and the paediatrician washed his hands.

Dr Donald complimented Josh on being so brave and left them to return to his patients. Ellie held a pad firmly over the puncture site for another twenty minutes until finally the nurse came back to check that Josh wasn't bleeding from the procedure.

The nurse lifted the dressing and appeared satisfied. She handed Ellie Josh's clothes. 'Josh can go, Mrs Diamond. The doctor will see you both again tomorrow at one o'clock in Bell's River. He's going to try and rush the pathologist first thing so that the results will be ready for you then.'

Ellie moistened her dry mouth and nodded. 'Thank you.' She just managed to get the words out past the lump in her throat. She held out her hand for Josh. 'Come on, darling, let's go home.'

The nurse added, 'Dr Donald also notified Dr Farrell as he was the referring doctor.'

Ellie shakily helped Josh with his clothes and they walked out into the corridor towards the exit. Her limbs felt stiff with tension and Ellie didn't know how she was going to get through the night.

CHAPTER TWELVE

WHEN Ellie turned into her driveway, Luke was waiting for them. She'd told him not to come. Thank goodness he hadn't listened.

Suddenly, the tears she'd tried to hold back seeped out of the corners of her eyes and trickled down her face. How had she ever thought she could do this without Luke?

As the car stopped he opened her door and she tumbled out into his arms and he hugged her to him and cradled her head.

'All right, sweetheart,' he soothed as she shuddered against his shirt for a moment before she gathered herself. Jerkily, she pulled out of his grasp and met his eyes briefly before moving to Josh's door. He lay slumped in his car seat, snoring softly after his traumatic day.

'I'll get him,' Luke said, and Ellie nodded as she unstrapped Josh and then stepped back for Luke to pick him up.

Ten minutes later, Josh was asleep in his bed and Ellie and Luke were sitting on the lounge. Ellie's head rested on Luke's shoulder.

'Today was horrific. Thank you for being here when I got home.' He squeezed her shoulder and didn't say anything.

'The doctor says it might be leukaemia.' She raised tortured eyes to his.

He squeezed her shoulder again. 'It's not definite.

Whatever it is, we'll get through Josh's illness together. I want to be with you in this, Ellie.'

She nudged him. 'You said you didn't want to see me again.' It was good to talk of something else, even for a few minutes, because she didn't think she could discuss the doctor's prognosis again just yet.

He looked at her. 'I was angry.' She felt him shrug against her shoulder. 'Shocked and confused and very, very angry—and you were the whipping boy. I'm sorry. If it's any consolation...' he smiled '...Travis wore it worse later.'

She could forget that now, but there were things she had to know.

'Why did Travis let everyone believe he was dead?'

Luke sighed. 'Amnesia. The day he went missing, he must have been hit by his surfboard or been knocked semi-conscious when he was dumped by a wave. He was picked up, floating on his board, about three miles out to sea by a fishing boat. They dropped him at the next port, which turned out to be in Coffs Harbour.'

'Why didn't they report finding him?'

'Apparently they weren't a strictly legal vessel and no one on board wanted to answer any questions. I'd say he was lucky they didn't just leave him to the sharks.'

'He couldn't remember his name and except for the slogan on his T-shirt, which he found familiar, he couldn't remember anything. Anyway, when he got off the boat, one of the young blokes was jumping ship with plans to work on an oil rig he'd heard about on the North-West Shelf. He convinced Travis to travel with him because the money was supposed to be phenomenal.'

Ellie shook her head. 'So when did he remember he had a wife and a family?'

'About a month later.' Luke shook his head in disbelief. 'June saw me this morning after she left the hospital and told me everything. He rang my office when he realised everyone must think he was dead, but I was up at the hospital. He asked June what was going on and she told him about the memorial service and that Belinda was coming to me for her antenatal care.'

He shook his head. 'That's when it got crazy. I didn't quite get whose idea it was for him to stay at the rig until just before the baby was born, but the idea was to raise enough money for some boatyard he'd fallen in love with and start a new life away from my mother with Belinda and the baby.'

'How could he do that to his wife?'

Luke shrugged. 'He said the damage had been done and he could see a way for good to come out of it. June kept him posted and as it got closer to the time he would come back, she was to drop hints to Belinda so that she wouldn't be destroyed when he did turn up. He honestly believed this was his last chance to break away before the baby was born.' He smiled wryly. 'He did save enough, incidentally.'

Ellie shook her head. She really didn't care. 'So why didn't they tell you?'

'Because he knew I wouldn't allow my mother to grieve a minute more than was necessary.' Luke shrugged. 'I know she has done some very cruel and selfish things in her time. Look what she did to us.' He met Ellie's eyes. 'And that's another apology we both owe you. She knows that I believe you. When I pressed her, she admitted to fabricating a wife for me. But she's still my mother and Travis knows I could strangle him if I weren't so glad he was alive.'

Ellie squeezed his hand. 'I'm sorry I couldn't tell you when I realised there was something going on.'

His arm tightened around her shoulder. 'No, I'm sorry. I should never have blamed you. They say you take things out on those that are closest to you and unfortunately you bore the brunt of my hurt at his actions.'

Ellie rested her head back on his shoulder. 'I'd promised Belinda and June I wouldn't break their trust. I hated those secrets between us.'

He soothed her and then he took her to bed. To hold and comfort until the morning brought answers to her biggest fear. But whatever the answer, he would be there for her.

'Please sit down, Mrs Diamond.' Dr Donald gestured to the chairs in front of his desk.

'Luke?' Ellie reached for his hand, although she was calmer now. It was right for Luke to be there. She didn't think she could listen to this without him. She needed a group hug before they did this. Ellie rested her forehead on his chest and she could feel Josh's tiny hand playing with her hair. She lifted her face to Luke and took a deep breath.

'All right. Let's hear what he has to say. The important thing is we're all together in this.'

They sat down to face the doctor and Ellie cuddled Josh on her lap as if to protect him.

'First of all...' Rob Donald paused and smiled at them all '...the bone-marrow biopsy clearly rules out leukaemia. As I said before, Josh's blood tests are back as well.'

Ellie started to shake with the reaction and Luke edged his chair right next to hers so he could slide his arm around her shoulder.

His warmth seeped into her slowly and the shaking settled a little.

The paediatrician went on, 'Josh's blood tests do indicate a very high leucocyte count and prolonged bleeding times consistent with my initial diagnosis.' He looked under his shaggy brows and with a gentle smile he looked at Ellie. 'I'd say young Josh is in that ten per cent we touched upon. He has an idiopathic—meaning from no specific cause—thrombocytopenia, perhaps triggered by the previous viral infection when he had the tummy bug.

'Basically, his body is producing an antibody that is coating the platelets—the bleeding stoppers—in his blood and making those platelets break down. The lack of platelets is what is making him bleed and the increase in white blood cells is what is making him tired.'

Ellie nodded. 'You said it's not leukaemia—which means he will get better? Is that right?'

The doctor nodded.

Ellie frowned. 'So you can treat it?' He nodded again. Ellie went on, 'How long before he starts to feel better?'

'I'll treat him with corticosteroids, which can cause a decrease in the production of the antibody and also decreases the spleen's efforts to get rid of the antibody-covered platelets. Plus, it will help his actual blood vessels not be so fragile to help stop them breaking and bruising.'

'And how long will he have to be on steroids?' Ellie hated the thought of Josh taking prednisone but it was worlds better than the chemotherapy she'd been dreading.

'For about a month. We'll have weekly blood tests to monitor his progress but it's up to you to keep him quiet and rested for the next few weeks. Encourage his appetite and see that he gets a little sun and lots of fluids.' Ellie nodded.

Josh had fallen asleep in Ellie's arms and Luke stood up and lifted him from her lap. He stood there with her son in his arms and Ellie struggled to her feet. 'Thank you, Doctor.' She shook the older man's hand and smiled tremulously at Luke.

'Let's go home.' He nodded and held the door open for her. She didn't know whether to laugh or cry—all she knew was she wanted to be at home before she did either.

An hour later, Josh lay asleep in his bed and Luke and Ellie sat together on the lounge. Her hand was in his and she sighed as she began to dare to believe that Josh would be fine.

Luke had been there with them, as he should have been, because he was a part of her and she couldn't hide from it any longer. It was her time to stop running. To accept that this was where she belonged, for ever. There were no greener pastures than this.

'I love you,' she whispered.

Luke stiffened beside her. Then his finger came down under her chin and lifted her face so that he could see it.

His eyes were filled with dawning hope and she felt the tears well in her own eyes because of all the pain she'd caused him.

'Now she tells me. Well, thank the Lord for that. I was beginning to think I'd never hear those words from you.'

Ellie leaned forward and allowed her lips to rest on his for a second as if to draw strength before moving back to stare at him. 'I've had a lot of problems coming to grips with it—but after today I've come to realise that everything in life is so uncertain, I'd better live it how I want to.' She didn't flinch. 'And I don't want to live without you ever again.'

He closed his eyes for a moment and when he opened them she could see herself reflected in his eyes. 'Then let's get married,' he said. 'Forget that offer I made about living together, it was never what I wanted. This week.

Next week. Soon. I'll look after you and Josh. You can work or not work, whatever you want. You'll be free to take the next few months off just to spend time with Josh.' He hugged her again.

'When Josh is better, the three of us will go away for a holiday to get some time for our family away from other people. How does that sound?'

It sounded like heaven to Ellie. 'Wonderful.' The emotions of the last few days crashed in on her. She felt too drained to move and she just sat there, drawing strength from Luke's arm around her. She knew in his mind he was making plans for their future. Like he always had. And this time she wasn't going anywhere.

CHAPTER THIRTEEN

THE wedding was held at the cove.

The beach was strewn with colourful market umbrellas dotting the sand and a hundred barefoot guests milled around, drinking champagne and congratulating the newly married couple. Louise Hollows, still pregnant, sipped juice and laughed with her friends. Everywhere babies and toddlers crawled and played and bigger children splashed in the rock pools.

Ellie walked hand in hand with her new husband and Luke's hand rested on their son's shoulder. Josh fidgeted with a surplus of energy as he looked enviously at the children playing in the edge of the waves.

'Off you go.' Ellie smiled. 'You've been very patient this last month and you're well now.'

Elsa and June sat together in an uneasy truce and both stood up as Ellie and Luke approached.

'Congratulations, both of you. It was an unconventional but beautiful wedding,' Luke's mother said.

June's eyes twinkled behind her glasses. 'Elsa and I have to get on now, for the sake of the grandchildren—isn't that right, Elsa?'

Elsa gave a faint smile in June's direction until her attention was taken by her granddaughter. Her lined face softened and she chucked the baby under her chin. 'She is adorable.'

Luke's mother looked over to where Belinda and Travis stared out to sea at their new boat moored off the breaker line. Then she turned to Ellie. 'I've been given another chance, and in the time I have left I hope I can make up for some of the mistakes I've made.'

Ellie allowed her cheek to be kissed and she met her mother-in-law's look with her own. She and Elsa had made good progress in understanding each other in the month since Ellie had agreed to be Luke's wife. And while she couldn't forget Elsa's selfish and destructive actions, Ellie was prepared to forgive her mother-in-law, for Luke's sake as much as anything else. 'Let all the bad things wash away,' she said. 'Starting afresh is a wonderful feeling.'

Elsa's eyes misted and Ellie barely heard her whisper, 'Thank you, my dear.'

Luke hugged his mother and then steered his wife towards their friends. It was the beginning of a whole new wonderful life and finally he had the woman he'd always wanted by his side. For ever.

Modern Romance™
...seduction and
passion guaranteed

Tender Romance™
...love affairs that
last a lifetime

Medical Romance™
...medical drama
on the pulse

Historical Romance™
...rich, vivid and
passionate

Sensual Romance™
...sassy, sexy and
seductive

Blaze Romance™
...the temperature's
rising

27 new titles every month.

Live the emotion

MILLS & BOON®

MILLS & BOON

Medical Romance™

TO THE DOCTOR A DAUGHTER by *Marion Lennox*

Dr Nate Ethan has all he needs – a job he loves as a country doctor and a bachelor lifestyle. Dr Gemma Campbell is about to change all that! Her sister has left her with two children – and one of them is Nate's. She must give Nate his baby and walk away – but Nate finds he will do anything to stop her leaving…

A MOTHER'S SPECIAL CARE by *Jessica Matthews*

Dr Mac Grant is struggling as a single dad with a demanding career. Juggling is proving difficult, and he is aware of his son's longing for a mother. Lori Ames is a nurse on Mac's ward – a single mother with a beautiful daughter of her own. Can she bestow upon them the special care that both children so desperately need?

RESCUING DR MacALLISTER by *Sarah Morgan*

A&E nurse Ellie Harrison is intrigued by the ruggedly handsome new doctor at Ambleside. But Dr Ben MacAllister is playing it cool. The pace and excitement of the A&E department thrusts them together and reveals that Ben's growing attraction is as strong as hers – then Ellie realises he has a secret…

On sale 2nd May 2003

Available at most branches of WH Smith, Tesco, Martins, Borders, Eason, Sainsbury's and all good paperback bookshops.

MILLS & BOON

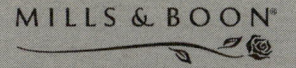

Medical Romance™

DR DEMETRIUS'S DILEMMA by *Margaret Barker*

Eight years ago Dr Demetrius Petros and Staff Nurse Chloe Metcalfe had a passionate affair on the beautiful Greek island of Ceres. It ended when a devastated Chloe returned to England, believing he had never really loved her. Now they are working together — and it's as if they have never been apart…

THE SURGEON'S GIFT by *Carol Marinelli*

Sister Rachael Holroyd has returned to Melbourne City hospital after a traumatic year away — yet the new plastic surgeon manages to make her heart flutter and she finds herself falling for him fast! Dr Hugh Connell is as gifted as he is gorgeous — and he just knows he can help Rachael get over her troubled past…

THE NURSE'S CHILD by *Abigail Gordon*

GP Richard Haslett isn't looking for a wife, and has promised his adopted daughter never to replace her mother. However, he finds himself drawn to Freya Farnham, the new Resident Nurse at Amelia's school. Then he discovers that Freya is Amelia's real mother…

On sale 2nd May 2003

Available at most branches of WH Smith, Tesco, Martins, Borders, Eason, Sainsbury's and all good paperback bookshops.

Margaret Way
Susan Fox
Jule McBride

With this Ring

An extra-special anthology
of three bridal short stories...

MILLS & BOON

Available from 18th April 2003

*Available at most branches of WH Smith,
Tesco, Martins, Borders, Eason, Sainsbury's
and all good paperback bookshops.*

0403/73/MB72

MILLS & BOON

DON'T MISS...

MILLS & BOON
BETTY NEELS
LAST APRIL FAIR
& THE COURSE OF TRUE LOVE

THE ULTIMATE COLLECTION

VOLUME TEN

On sale 4th April 2003

Available at most branches of WH Smith, Tesco, Martins, Borders, Eason, Sainsbury's and all good paperback bookshops.

2 FREE
books and a surprise gift!

We would like to take this opportunity to thank you for reading this Mills & Boon® book by offering you the chance to take TWO more specially selected titles from the Medical Romance™ series absolutely FREE! We're also making this offer to introduce you to the benefits of the Reader Service™—

- ★ FREE home delivery
- ★ FREE gifts and competitions
- ★ FREE monthly Newsletter
- ★ Exclusive Reader Service discount
- ★ Books available before they're in the shops

Accepting these FREE books and gift places you under no obligation to buy, you may cancel at any time, even after receiving your free shipment. Simply complete your details below and return the entire page to the address below. *You don't even need a stamp!*

YES! Please send me 2 free Medical Romance books and a surprise gift. I understand that unless you hear from me, I will receive 4 superb new titles every month for just £2.60 each, postage and packing free. I am under no obligation to purchase any books and may cancel my subscription at any time. The free books and gift will be mine to keep in any case.

M3ZEA

Ms/Mrs/Miss/Mr ....Initials...................................
BLOCK CAPITALS PLEASE

Surname ....

Address ....

....

....Postcode................................

Send this whole page to:
UK: FREEPOST CN81, Croydon, CR9 3WZ
EIRE: PO Box 4546, Kilcock, County Kildare (stamp required)

Offer valid in UK and Eire only and not available to current Reader Service subscribers to this series. We reserve the right to refuse an application and applicants must be aged 18 years or over. Only one application per household. Terms and prices subject to change without notice. Offer expires 31st July 2003. As a result of this application, you may receive offers from Harlequin Mills & Boon and other carefully selected companies. If you would prefer not to share in this opportunity please write to The Data Manager at the address above.

Mills & Boon® is a registered trademark owned by Harlequin Mills & Boon Limited.
Medical Romance™ is being used as a trademark.